Full Circle

Paige Kin

CHAPTER ONE

Today it smelled like worms. It was the second day of constant drizzle and mist. The leaf-strewn ground was downright soggy. All the worms had crawled out of their drowned homes, their little naked pink and gray bodies looking vulnerable and exposed. Anna was driving her younger daughter to preschool and her older daughter to elementary school. In the midst of her routine errands, Anna tried to take pleasure in the November splendor all around her. Somehow on these gray, damp days the autumn golds, reds and oranges glowed even richer than on a sunny day. Her drive from Lucy's preschool on Plank Road to Martha's elementary school on Lorraine Avenue took her past horse farms and through winding neighborhoods. The trees were at the tail end of peak color, straining to produce their most brilliant hue before releasing a final sigh and falling to the ground.

"Do I look pretty, Momma?" Lucy asked, pushing against her car seat straps to try and see herself in the rearview mirror.

"Yes, dear," Anna responded for about the tenth time that morning. On an ordinary day Lucy cared a great deal about her appearance, much more than her mother or sister cared about theirs. Today, however, she was having a tea party at preschool and had actually been instructed to dress up. A painstaking search through Martha's hand-me-downs resulted in Lucy producing the perfect party dress, as well as a trashed bedroom. Stepping over the piles of unsuitable clothing, Lucy proudly announced, "This is the one, Momma! With my white tights, tall black shoes, and I want braids..." Anna had to admit, her four year old did have good fashion sense. And, in spite of her motherly prejudice, she knew Lucy truly was quite pretty. Her long, champagne-colored hair and huge blue/green eyes were going to break a lot of hearts some day. They were also going to cause Adam, Anna's husband, to go prematurely gray. Lucy had been compared by more than one person to Goldie Hawn, not just in looks, but in personality as well. Even at four years old it was clear: Lucy was a force to be reckoned with.

Anna glanced in the rearview mirror at Lucy's choice of the forest green velvet dress with a wide satin waistband and bow.

"You look lovely, sweetheart. Very grown up!" Anna commended. Lucy beamed. Turning to Martha, she asked hopefully, "Do I look like a kindergartener-er?"

Martha giggled, "Yeah, Lucy, you could pass for five or even six years old!"

At that moment Anna pulled up in front of Lucy's preschool. One of the teacher's aides came out to the car to undo Lucy's seatbelt and walk her inside. Out on the pavement Lucy carefully smoothed her skirt before donning her oversized backpack. Stuffed mostly with napping supplies, such as a small pillow and blanket, her backpack was almost as big as she was. All of the preschoolers looked like tortoises with gigantic shells. It seemed as if a gust of wind would leave them helpless on their backs, with little arms and legs flailing. Anna pulled away from the school, waving to Lucy, who was busily chatting with the teacher's aide, no doubt fishing for compliments about her outfit. Merging her silver hatchback in with traffic, Anna suggested, "Do you want to practice your subtraction?"

"Oh, right," Martha agreed enthusiastically.

"Okay, what's fifteen minus eleven?" Anna quizzed. She managed to throw questions to Martha, concentrate on driving and at the same time contemplate her older daughter. Martha was so sweet, patient, loving and eager to please that sometimes it broke Anna's heart. When Anna was at the end of her rope and Lucy was still making demands, Martha would offer to play Barbies with Lucy (which she detested). If Anna and Adam were stressing over finances, Martha would empty her piggy bank. She was an asthmatic eight year old who wore glasses, got straight A's and was a Girl Scout. Somehow, though, she inspired not pity or teasing from classmates, but admiration. She possessed an inner strength and self-assurance that Anna envied even as an adult. Martha had always known her own mind--she didn't like dolls or make-up or princessy things. Her passions were wildlife, books and knowledge. Martha never pretended to be something she wasn't, and even her elementary-aged pals seemed to respect it. That, along with the fact that she was equally nice and attentive to everyone, meant she was perpetually surrounded by friends. Martha didn't have the movie-star looks of Goldie Hawn, but with her long, wheat-toned hair, gray/blue eyes and peaches-and-cream complexion, Anna had no worries that one day her elder daughter would also have a string of admirers.

"Mom, I said twelve. Is that right? Twenty-two minus ten?" Martha asked, penetrating Anna's musings.

"Oh, yes, that's right!" Anna said, pulling into the elementary school drop-off lane. "Well, here we are, dear." Martha collected her backpack and lunch sack before exiting the car.

"Bye, Momma!"

"Bye! Good luck on your quiz!" Anna called after her. Martha was already hurrying into the building. She never wanted to be late.

As Anna steered the Hyundai out of the parking lot and headed for the YMCA, she indulged in a huge sigh. Why did she feel heavy and burdened? Why, on a rich November day, Anna's favorite time of year, could she only seem to notice the smell of worms? She supposed it may have had something to do with her sister's baby shower the day before. There were always those gathering--weddings, funerals, New Year's Eve parties, and apparently baby showers that cause you to take stock of your life. Anna had found hers wanting.

There was no reason not to be perfectly happy. Anna had enjoyed eleven years of a happy marriage and was looking forward to decades more of Adam's companionship. She was blessed with two healthy, lovely children. Her husband was a new family practice doctor, after years of schooling and struggle. Even though finances were tight, Anna was able to stay home and raise her children herself. Shouldn't she be content? Shouldn't all of that be enough?

Anna slowed to a stop at a red light. Glancing in her rearview mirror, she noticed the man behind her watching his wipers. A wet leaf was trapped under his wiper, being dragged left-to-right, right-to-left. It was annoying the driver, whose frowning eyes tracked the leaf back and forth like a volleying ball at a tennis match. Anna was relieved when the light changed and she could pull away. The leaf was beginning to annoy her, too. As she approached the YMCA, strip malls, gas stations and drug stores quickly gave way to open fields, farm houses and family-owned restaurants and garages. The city of Fredericksburg, Virginia, where Anna lived, was expanding rapidly. Shops, chain restaurants and overpriced HOA controlled neighborhoods were popping

8

up with alarming speed. It made her think of the ever popular chia pet--just water and watch it grow! Still, sandwiched between Washington D.C. and Richmond, with fifty miles on each side, Fredericksburg quickly opened up into farmland. The YMCA Anna frequented Mondays, Wednesdays and Fridays when both girls were in school, was located in Massaponax, a rural area just south of Fredericksburg. It was a little further than she'd like to drive, but the facilities were bright and clean, and she knew after years of experimenting that she would only get a good workout if she went to a gym. She'd tried jogging, workout videos and an at-home treadmill. Like business professionals who could get more done at the office than working from home, Anna found she only took her workouts seriously if she went to her 'place of business.'

She negotiated the Hyundai into a small parking spot between a minivan and a SUV. These days driving a compact car was like being a beetle moving among brontosauruses. Anna grabbed her gym bag and purse and exited the car. Hurrying through the drizzle, she entered the YMCA, flashed her member card and headed for the locker room. Within a few minutes her belongings

9

were safely locked away and Anna was working up a sweat on the elliptical machine.

Gazing at her bobbing figure in the wall of mirrors facing her, Anna began pumping her legs harder. She wasn't pleased with her reflection. She was okay with her dark blonde hair. At the moment it was pulled back in a ponytail and her bangs were lying flat against her forehead. When she took time with a curling iron though, it could look quite attractive, hanging to her shoulders in blonde waves. She also liked her smoky-blue eyes which were framed by dark lashes and eyebrows. Not wanting to fuss with her contacts, though, they were hidden by gold-framed glasses. What she was truly not happy with was that she still needed to lose twenty-to-thirty pounds to be a healthy weight to fit her petite 5'2" frame. Anna had put on fifteen pounds or so in her first three years of marriage--that typical time of settling in, getting comfortable and no longer trying to impress anyone. But she had really tacked on the weight while pregnant with Martha. In retrospect, Anna felt it was due to having a difficult time conceiving. She and Adam had tried for over a year before Anna got pregnant. Once it finally happened, she wanted to immediately look

10

pregnant, feel pregnant and enjoy all the indulgences of being pregnant. So, she threw caution to the wind and ate anything she wanted. That was almost nine years ago, and she was still trying to get the weight off.

Pumping her arms and legs, Anna glanced down at the 'calories' gauge. She'd burned 100 calories so far-- halfway done! Her goal was to burn 200 calories in approximately 20 to 25 minutes. When she first joined the gym three months before her goal had been 150 calories, so at least she was making progress. 'Now,' Anna thought, 'what to ponder for these last ten minutes?' The elliptical machine created almost a bicycling motion, except standing. Therefore, it was virtually impossible to read, or even look at magazine pictures without getting dizzy or developing a headache. There were five wall-mounted TV's facing the machines, but you had to read the closed captioning to follow what was going on. Besides, all the TV's were on news or sports channels.

So, Anna's thoughts drifted back to her sister's baby shower. Anna and Faith were identical twins. Even with Anna in Fredericksburg and Faith an hour away in Richmond, the two were inseparable. They had always been best friends. After leaving home they were

11

roommates in college, pursued the same major and even entered the same graduate studies. They only separated when each got married. They joked that if they out-lived their husbands, they would move in together and end their days as they had begun. Whereas Anna had started her family at age 24, Faith had waited until now, at 33. Anna was truly thrilled--she'd been waiting for a little niece or nephew to spoil. The excitement was bittersweet, though. Anna couldn't help noting that at the time of Faith's baby shower she was supposed to have had a newborn of her own. The previous January Anna had been delighted to realize that she was pregnant. In eleven years of marriage she and Adam had practiced virtually no birth control (besides the stretches of abstinence during some of his toughest med school and residency schedules). Still, they had only two children to show for it. They had actually begun looking into adoption just before Lucy was finally conceived. Obviously, something physiological was going on, but since they were, eventually, able to conceive, they decided not to pursue the problem. Anna had been about to give up on a third child when she finally conceived. Once pregnant, Anna had never had any trouble carrying a healthy child. So, they had told the

12

girls the news and were thinking of names. Martha was reading <u>What to Expect When You're Expecting</u>. Then, at around eleven weeks, Anna miscarried. It was a devastating disappointment. Not two months later came the big announcement that Faith was pregnant. The crib, infant car seat and baby swing that Anna had begun pulling out of the basement and cleaning up to reuse were then ushered to Faith's house. Anna did her best to swallow her grief and be genuinely happy for and supportive of her sister. She had even painted the nursery and helped to plan, organize and make food for the shower.

Watching her sister admire the receiving blankets, bottles and crib sheets that signified the new beginning in Faith's life made Anna wonder about her own. She, also, felt she was at a place of beginnings. She just wasn't sure what she was supposed to be doing! She was 33 years old and had reached a crossroads. She finally had three days when the kids were in school, and next fall both girls would be at school all week. She had done odd jobs to help Adam get through med school and residency, but now he was finally building his own practice and Anna didn't have to look for employment.

She could actually catch her breath after years of caring for young children at home and a stressed, absent husband. So, what next? She had thought that having a third child was the answer. With that door closed, Anna felt lost.

Ending on that thought, she practically fell off the elliptical machine. With her thoughts going a mile a minute, she'd been unconsciously pedaling furiously. She'd burned 220 calories in 21 minutes! Feeling flushed and wobbly, she tried to look cool as she wiped down the machine and moved to the weight section on shaky legs. Thirty minutes later Anna emerged from the locker room, freshened and changed with sore muscles, but proud of herself. She had exchanged her sweat suit for a comfortable pair of jeans and a long-sleeve mock turtleneck in a flattering shade of brick red. After replenishing her lipstick, fluffing her bangs and twisting her hair up in a tortoise shell clip, Anna pronounced herself acceptable. She'd mostly avoided mirrors these past eight years since gaining all the weight. Normally after working out, she simply ran errands and did housework before picking Lucy up from school. Today, though, she had arranged to meet her close friend,

Barbara, for coffee and chit-chat. In the past eight years and ten months, since becoming a mother, Anna had enjoyed very little adult conversation and companionship. She feared her intellect and vocabulary had atrophied in all that time. In adult company Anna had to remember to say 'restroom' instead of 'potty' and restrain herself from not only unwrapping other's straws and cutting their meat, but also from praising them when they did it successfully themselves. If Anna did commit any such faux pas, however, Barbara would be the first to understand, as a mother herself of three children, ages 12, 8 and 5.

......"So, why, again, are you letting Chris get a mohawk?!" Anna asked incredulously. She and Barbara were settled comfortably with their pumpkin spice coffees at a table in the cafe of a bookstore. Barbara, who also loved fall, was sporting an attractive burnt orange sweater, tan slacks and a leaf-spattered scarf. Her build was similar to Anna's. She had gray/green eyes and light brown hair cut short, in a modern spiky style.

After sipping her coffee, Barbara sighed, "Well, you know we've been struggling to get Chris to pay attention and work hard in his classes. At home I can stay on him about homework and studying, but what can I do

15

if he's goofing off in the classroom?" Anna nodded. She knew Chris's trouble wasn't that he wasn't bright, but that he was brilliant. Twelve-year-old Chris was a whiz at math and computers, played the piano and was on the basketball team and in every accelerated class the school offered. Still, his grades didn't always reflect his genius. He got bored in class and would pass the time using his cleverness to entertain his classmates.

"Well," Barbara continued, "Chris had said this summer that he wanted a mohawk, and at the time I absolutely refused. Then, a month ago he came home with his interim report card and I knew we had to do something. I made a bet with him that I thought he could never win. I told him if he raised all of his grades to A's or B's by the first true report card time, then he could get a mohawk."

"Oh no," Anna giggled, guessing the rest of the story.

Barbara gave a strained, resigned smile. "I figure his grades are more important, right? Hair grows back."

"I can't wait to see this year's Christmas card!" Anna teased. She was once again actually quite

16

impressed with Barbara. Anna often thought her friend should give lessons in parenting. She was the 'Martha Stewart' of motherhood and homemaking, yet with more of a 'Roseanne Barr' down-to-earth approach. Anna found it refreshing to see a mother--especially a stay-at-home mom, who was realistic about parenting. Anna was so tired of encountering those yuppie, idealistic thirty-something stay-at-home moms (they usually moved about in groups) who had their parenting priorities all wrong. Parenting for them was a keeping-up-with-the-Joneses kind of affair, all about appearances. Their kids must eat organic foods, be pushed about in Eddie Bauer strollers, attend playgroups, participate in swimming, dancing or music lessons, host catered birthday parties and be reading by age four. The mothers also had to fit certain criteria: they generally drove minivans or SUV's, weighed no more than 130 pounds with salon styled and colored hair, lived in houses with a separate playroom and a magazine-style kitchen, volunteered at a school, church or charity and were a member of some mom's group. For them, the goal had become how many accomplishments could be listed on some imaginary resume rather than simply raising decent kids. Having grown up in the very

17

antithesis of 'yuppy-ville', Anna knew that what kids really needed was simply a stable home life that they could count on, along with lots of love and laughter.

"Enough about me," Barbara said, interrupting Anna's thoughts, "How was your sister's baby shower?"

"It was nice," Anna responded noncommittally. She slowly drank the last of her coffee, aware that Barbara was studying her intently.

"I'm sorry, Anna. I should have thought--I mean, that party can't have been easy for you," Barbara sympathized.

"It really wasn't so much the miscarriage--at least, not as bad as I thought. I just, well, I guess I feel a little lost now, you know?"

"You and Adam can always keep trying."

"Well, it's not exactly about another child in particular. I mean, I'd be basically okay if we were done having kids. It's more about what I want to do with my life now," Anna said slowly. She was always reluctant to voice her feelings of restlessness and boredom to other stay-at-home mothers. She didn't want to imply that home-making alone wasn't challenging. She certainly

18

knew firsthand what a crock that was! But, for whatever reason, it had never been enough for Anna.

"You've got the days now that Lucy's in preschool. You could volunteer somewhere or get a part-time job," Barbara suggested.

"Yes, I know," Anna sighed, "we could certainly use the extra money. I guess I'm just being idealistic, but I don't want something to fill the hours. I want something that I really care about. I mean, shouldn't life be about more than just getting through each day?"

To Anna's surprise, Barbara responded, "Yeah, I know what you mean. I've actually been feeling the same way lately."

"Really? I thought you were happy at home."

"I am, but I think I'm ready for more. I'm 35 years old, Anna. My kids are all in school now. They're just going to continue getting older and begin lives of their own."

"Exactly!" Anna agreed, "I want a new beginning in my life."

"Well, here's to new beginnings," said Barbara, raising her cup and draining the last of the coffee.

Anna glanced at her watch. "Oh, I better get out of here. I've got to get a few groceries before I pick up Lucy."

"Do you want to get together on Friday?" Barbara offered, gathering her coat and purse.

"Yeah, that sounds good. I'm going to make myself begin going through all the junk in the basement tomorrow. It's going to take a couple days to even get to the point where I can walk around down there! I'll need a break by Friday."

"Okay, good luck!" Barbara said, hugging her friend quickly before heading out.

"Thanks!"

CHAPTER TWO

Standing knee deep in Christmas ornaments, beach balls, coolers and motor oil, Anna had a sudden inspiration--why not just bag up the entire mess and call AMVETS? Would the family really miss any of this junk? 'We could turn this room into a rec room!' she thought wildly. Then she noticed the stained concrete floor, exposed insulation and pipes, all dimly lit by a bare ceiling bulb. "Maybe not," Anna mumbled to herself. Gazing about in despair with a trash bag in one hand and a lone mitten in the other, she wondered if it was possible to 'accidentally' burn everything in only one room without reducing the entire house to ashes. "I think I need a break," Anna muttered, realizing she was actually turning to thoughts of arson. Climbing over piles of a decade's worth of family life, she finally made her way out of the storage room. After switching off the light and firmly closing the door behind her, she climbed the stairs up to the living area. She and Adam had bought this townhouse somewhat out of desperation a year and a half ago when he finished residency. Moving from the rural, western part of Virginia to the northern area within commuting

21

distance of D.C. had been quite a culture shock. Everything, especially real estate, cost three times more. Being unable to afford a decent home in a decent area, Anna and Adam had bought a newly built three-story townhouse. Anna missed the large yard they had before, but she enjoyed the modern amenities that had been glaringly absent in their former little 1959 brick ranch. Before, Anna had tried to cook for her family in a galley-style kitchen no bigger than a walk-in closet. There was no dishwasher, no garbage disposal, and the stove was older than she was. The repairman who came out to fix the oven door told Anna the stove was 40 years old. He was impressed that it was still working, but warned her that if any of the elements started dying, they didn't make replacement parts for it anymore. His comment sent Anna's thoughts whirling, like a plot of some cheesy murder mystery. Maybe she could kill the stove and make it look accidental! She could sabotage the stove herself so they could replace it with a new one! But she quickly reconsidered, knowing that on Adam's resident salary they couldn't afford a new one. The stove was still going strong when they moved three years later.

Sometimes Anna wondered if the new lady of that house was also plotting a stove 'accident.'

The new townhouse came complete with all new kitchen appliances, including a dishwasher, disposal, stove, fridge and built-in microwave. Unlike the small, dark interior of the ranch house, the townhouse had 6' x 6' windows and sliding glass doors that let in plenty of sunlight. Besides the three bedrooms, open living, dining and kitchen area and the downstairs den with a walkout patio, the townhouse boasted 3 1/2 baths! They had come from a house with one bathroom so small that if they all were inside at one time, someone would have to step in the tub in order to pull the door inward to open it. Of course, when it came time to clean, she wasn't as thrilled by the four toilets.

Anna had little-to-no complaints about the interior of the townhouse. She was, however, getting tired of the issues surrounding the exterior. For instance, their large front window looked out onto what was essentially a parking lot. Also, the houses were so squashed together that from the kitchen window the girls could talk to friends two doors down in their backyard. Living at such close quarters, you couldn't help but be

23

very aware of whom your neighbors were--Anna wasn't so thrilled with some of hers. Thankfully, the people occupying the houses immediately adjacent to hers were fine. But teenagers tended to loiter around with nothing to do but look for trouble. There had been one break-in and one drug bust that Anna knew of. In her naivety, Anna had assumed that with such expensive, new townhouses only hard-working professionals would be moving in. What she hadn't considered were investors planning to buy the homes and then rent them to most anyone. The neighborhood was brand new, and it hadn't yet turned completely 'bad' or 'good.' Anna couldn't tell which direction it was headed. She dreamed of moving out to some remote area where she and her family could live peacefully. Financially, though, such a move was out of the question.

So, for the moment she tried to enjoy the interior of her home, shutting out the rest. She tended to leave the blinds on the windows facing the other town homes mostly closed, with the rear, forest-facing window blinds wide open. It was this view she took in while standing in the kitchen waiting for the kettle to boil. She was immensely grateful for the dense woods directly behind

24

the townhouse. Gazing at the trees gave her peace. She was determined that one day she would be in a home that offered such a view from every window.

The shriek of the kettle tore Anna from her reverie. She pulled her favorite Laura Ashley mug from the cabinet. It was a delicate, lightweight cup in a cream tone covered in tiny blue and pink flowers. She dropped in an orange spice teabag and filled it with steaming water. Waiting for the tea to steep, she located a box of gingersnaps and emptied a few onto a plate. After considering it a moment, Anna also proceeded to make Lucy a cup of tea. She could hear Lucy playing in her bedroom above, but she knew as soon as she settled in to her cup, Lucy would appear, demanding her own. It never failed.

Anna carefully carried a tray with the two mugs and plate of cookies to the coffee table. Just as she settled on the couch and took a sip of her steaming tea, Lucy trundled downstairs asking, "What are you drinking, Momma?"

Anna smiled to herself--Lucy radar strikes again! "It's hot tea. Here's some for you," Anna offered.

"'Kay!" Lucy agreed, blowing on her tea and reaching for a cookie.

"What have you been doing?" Anna asked, trying to get her mind off of the mess waiting for her in the basement.

"I been doin' my work," Lucy answered importantly.

Anna smiled to herself again. Lucy had been disappointed that her mom planned to work in the basement today--a task Lucy couldn't really help with. Not to be outdone, Lucy had created some crucial work of her own.

"How's your work going?" Anna inquired, nibbling on a gingersnap.

Lucy sighed, "Not really good. Sam keeps bothering me. I tried to write in my notebook and do my calc'lator. But, he just wants me to play with him." Anna made sympathetic sounds. Sam was Lucy's imaginary brother. The fact that he appeared just after Anna's miscarriage was not, she believed, a coincidence. It always have her a little 'guilt jolt' when Sam was mentioned, even though she knew intellectually that she was not at fault.

26

"I don't wanna work anymore," Lucy declared, after a careful sip of her tea. To Lucy, any beverage that was a touch above lukewarm was too hot to drink. She preferred her hot tea and hot chocolate tepid.

"Do you want to take a break and watch something?" Anna suggested, "I can stay in here for awhile with you and go through boxes."

"'Kay!" Lucy agreed, glad of her mother's company. She headed for the TV armoire and opened the drawer containing the children's DVD's. After careful consideration she chose a Disney Princess Sing-a-long collection. Anna inwardly groaned, but kept her mouth shut. If Martha had been there, she would have rolled her eyes and run upstairs with her hands over her ears.

"I want this one, Mommy," Lucy said thrusting the very pink case at Anna. "And, can I have play-dough?"

Ten minutes later Lucy was busy sculpting a blue play-dough masterpiece and Anna sat facing a box stuffed full of papers. She had pulled three such boxes out of the basement. She wanted to be able to sit comfortably while she sorted through old receipts, Christmas cards, insurance papers, and who knew what

27

else. She knew the only way she'd make herself pick through all that mess was by leaving it out where she'd keep tripping over it. So, with Pocahontas singing about 'Colors in the Wind' in the background, Anna began sifting through the papers. Some she shredded, others were set aside to file later, and any keepsakes like cards or drawings were piled for scrapbooking.

Anna mentally chastised herself for putting off this task for so long. There were things here from when Martha was in preschool! Still, she thought she shouldn't be too hard on herself. For the past seven years Adam had been in medical school and residency, rarely at home and rarely conscious when he was home. Anna had been raising two young children and trying everything from crafting, babysitting and decorating to make extra money. There hadn't been a lot of time or energy remaining for things such as filing. Humming along with 'Someday My Prince Will Come,' Anna pushed aside a receipt for a medical text (\$150 for Obstetrics and Adam didn't even do any deliveries anymore!) and a Christmas pageant program from Martha's 3 year old preschool class. She was trying to get to something gold at the bottom of the box. Frowning, she finally wrestled a gold-toned journal from under the clutter. "What's this?" Anna muttered.

"It's a magical unicorn dragon!" Lucy answered proudly, pointing to her vaguely animal-shaped play-dough creation. Glancing up, Anna responded distractedly, "Oh, yes, sweetie, that's....good."

"What's that book, Mommy?" Lucy asked, eyes always alert to anything sparkly.

"Well, I'm not sure. I just found it," Anna answered, turning the journal slowly in her hands. There was nothing written on the outside. Lucy sidled up next to her mother as she opened the cover. On the inside, written in spindly cursive was *'Annie McDowell 1948 THOUGHTS'.*

"Is it a magical treasure?" Lucy wondered hopefully.

"It just may be," Anna answered slowly. "This is a journal written by your great-grandmother, the one I'm named after. She died soon after Daddy and I were married. I forgot I had this."

"Oh," Lucy said, her interest beginning to fade once she realized the golden book wasn't going to speak or sing or even spill open with glowing colors. Nothing in real life was as wonderful as in Disney movies. Lucy returned to her play-dough and watched Belle singing about loving the Beast.

Anna, on the other hand, felt as if she had just walked into a Disney scene. To her, the golden journal was magical. It had appeared after years of dormancy to speak truths to her about her grandmother, a woman she'd always greatly admired. Growing up, Anna and Faith had spent weeks during their summer vacations with their grandmother. She had been a widow for years and yearned for the company. More than that, though, she adored her twin granddaughters, and they did her. Annie McDowell was not a typical grandmother--that is, she wasn't frail, she didn't rant about 'kids these days', and she didn't have blue hair. She was a tiny little 5' blonde (thanks to Clairol), bursting with nervous energy. At home she always wore navy or tan slacks with sensible tennis shoes and a top that disguised her wrinkled neck and flabby upper arms. On Sundays she wore a rose-colored suit that complemented her fair skin and a modest skirt that showed off her still-shapely calves (of which she was inwardly proud). She dressed, not to meet other's expectations of someone her age, but to accentuate her

30

best features. She often sighed and resigned herself to the limited selection of clothes that still looked good on her elderly body. She was endlessly interested in the newest fashions for the young, but had the good sense to not try and sport them herself. Annie McDowell had a great sense of style (maybe that's where Lucy gets her fashion sense, thought Anna). Annie had once told her granddaughters that she would have loved being an interior decorator, if she had been born in an era when women had both families and careers. Instead, she married and began her family when she was only a teenager herself. She remained dependent on her husband as she raised two children and took in ironing and sewing to make extra money. When he passed away, Annie found herself in her 50's with little social security, no job and unable to drive a car or even write a check. With the help of family and friends, she learned all of those things and got a job at K-Mart. Living simply, she managed to work and support herself to retirement age. Then, at age 70 she snagged herself a husband. Anna would never forget her grandmother telling her how she schemed to gain the attention of Joseph, a man she'd known for years before and met again at a funeral! Anna would also never

31

forget her grandmother showing her a black satin nightgown she'd bought for the honeymoon! Go Granny! Annie and Joseph enjoyed fifteen happy years together before they died, within a year of each other.

Looking closer at the date on the journal, Anna realized that her grandmother was around her age when she wrote it. All Anna wanted to do was sit before a flickering fire with a pot of freshly brewed tea and read the entire journal from beginning to end. However, considering she didn't even own a fireplace, her tea had grown cold and the last Disney princess was belting out the notes of the final song on Lucy's DVD, her prospects seemed dim. With a sigh, Anna carefully placed the journal on her desk to enjoy later. She simply couldn't bear the thought of returning to the boxes, much less the mess in the basement. She quickly gathered together the piles of papers and boxes, shoving them all into a hidden corner of the dining room. "This stuff's been floating around for seven years. It can wait another day or two," Anna said to no one in particular.

"Mommy, I'm tired of play-dough," complained Lucy.

"Come on," said Anna, suddenly desperate to get out of the house. "Let's clean up this play-dough and go to the park."

"Yeah!" cheered Lucy, as she demolished her colorful sculptures.

"I'll give Miss Charlotte a call and see if little Charlie and Emma can meet us," offered Anna. Something about finding the journal made Anna feel restless. Maybe it had to do with the reminder that time was so fleeting. When Annie McDowell had written that journal, she'd been young, with small children at home. Now her life was over and those children were grandparents themselves. Anna suddenly felt a real need to enjoy her youth and play with Lucy while her little girl still cared about playing.

.... "...and so, her head began to really stink, so I thought I'd better take her to the doctor," Charlotte continued her story while pushing 18 month-old Emma in the baby swing.

"Her head stunk?!" asked Anna, trying to hide her amusement.

33

"Yeah, really bad. That's when I knew that Emma hadn't eaten her peas; she'd stuck them up her nose."

"How did they get them out?" asked Anna, suppressing a giggle.

"They tried getting her to blow them out, but when that didn't work, they used these tweezer things....Charlie, don't climb up the slide.....Emma screamed bloody murder," Charlotte concluded. "So, anyway, what's been up with you?"

"Well, nothing as interesting as you!" Anna laughed, inwardly, she was thinking 'thank goodness!' Anna had known Charlotte for six years and never in that time had Charlotte's days been anything less than eventful. At barely 5' tall, Charlotte was a very chipper tiny whirling dervish. She had fair skin, straight blonde hair and twinkling blue eyes with deep laugh lines. She always had a smile ready at her lips. When Anna first med her, Charlotte was hugely pregnant, waddling as quickly as she could after her 60 pound Labrador. Anna and two-year-old Martha had been nearly run over by the two of them while playing on the sidewalk. Anna had never befriended anyone quite like Charlotte. She was always going in three directions at once, yet somehow managed to keep Anna centered. They were the best of friends for the one year that they were neighbors in Norfolk, Virginia. Charlotte's husband, David, was in the military, and Adam had been in medical school. After that brief year, David got orders to relocate, and Adam started his residency in Roanoke, Virginia. The women had remained long-distance friends, though, and six years later found themselves both living in Fredericksburg! Adam had joined a practice there, and David commuted up to the Quantico marine base.

"Charlie, I said don't climb up the slide!" Charlotte yelled while trying to free Emma from the baby swing.

"Lucy, make sure you don't slide down 'till Charlie's off, okay?" Anna called, seeing a potential collision about to take place. In theory, mothers took their kids to the playground for the children to get exercise while the parents relaxed and chatted. In practice, however, the mothers ended up running around as much as the kids, either playing referee or trying to act as a human safety net. Charlotte got more exercise than most. Emma was like a little wind-up doll. It seemed that

35

her chubby little legs were in walking motion even before she was placed on the ground. She truly had the features of a fine porcelain doll as well--ivory skin, large blue eyes with black lashes and curly hair the color of vanilla ice cream. Charlie had the same hair color, but with chocolate brown eyes. He, also, was in constant motion. He had just turned five and would be in kindergarten next year. Anna knew Charlotte was counting the days! Of course, she still had several years before both kids were in school. With a little jolt, Anna realized how big her own kids were getting. This time next year she'd have five entire days to herself! Instead of being excited, Anna felt a bit panicked. She always figured she'd find what she wanted to do with her life later, when the kids were older. Suddenly 'later' was becoming now!

As if reading her thoughts, Charlotte asked, "So, how's it been with Lucy in preschool this year? What have you been doing with all that free time?" Anna cringed inside. Here was the moment when she wanted to be able to share world-changing or at least life-changing work she'd taken on. How she longed to answer, "Oh, I'm making thousands of dollars from my home-based business," or "I've begun a fund that's raised millions for

36

cancer research." She wanted to feel that her free time had a purpose--something productive, creative and lucrative. Instead, she answered rather pathetically, "Well, I've been going to the YMCA."

Charlotte looked at her friend closely. "That's great, Anna. Why the sad tone in your voice?"

Anna sighed. "Because besides exercising and maybe getting groceries, I haven't been doing anything."

"That's not a bad thing. You've been raising kids full time for years, not to mention babysitting and decorating and crafting! You deserve some time of doing nothing."

Anna sighed again. She knew Charlotte was right. Anna had always pushed herself hard--valedictorian of her high school class, Phi Beta Kappa at William and Mary, and top of her graduate class before she quit to stay home with Martha. It was hard to give herself a break, even when she really needed it.

"I know, you're right. It's just, the girls started school in August, and now it's November. At what point does 'doing nothing' move from a deserved reward to simple laziness?" Anna spoke her fears aloud.

"Anna!" Charlotte laughed, "You're the least lazy person I've ever met!"

"What I mean is that this isn't a brief vacation-- this is only the beginning of more and more time of my own," Anna clarified.

"But, you make it sound like a prison sentence. Aren't you excited? I know I can't wait to have even an hour that's not already decided for me."

"I would be excited, if I had some sort of work that I was excited about. I know I sound ungrateful. I know there are so many moms out there who would give anything to have more of a choice about how they spent their days--and to be home when their kids got off the bus."

"Well, it sounds to me like you're in the ideal position. You can be there for the kids when they need you, and you can fill your free time any way you choose. You just need to explore what you enjoy doing," Charlotte summed up. Anna began to feel a little foolish. The way Charlotte put things made Anna think she was complaining about nothing. Maybe her supposed dilemma really was simple. Then why didn't it feel that way?

38

"Anna, you've spent so many years taking care of everyone else--all mothers do. You just need to allow yourself to get used to the idea of putting you first this time."

.... Charlotte's words kept running through Anna's head that evening as she puttered in the kitchen, preparing dinner. She knew her friend's advice was sound. Still, all these 'buts' kept popping up every time she tried to put herself first. Chopping potatoes and apples for a pork roast, Anna came back, again, to her original thought that she should probably be looking for a part-time job. Anna and Adam were trying to get out from under a mountain of debt--car loans, credit cards, school loans and a heavy mortgage. They were proud they had married young, started a family and gotten their educations without having to move in with their parents or give up their dreams. Still, it had come at a high financial price. Over the years Anna had done childcare in her home and amateur interior decorating to help pay the bills. But, before now there had never been any question of a true job--the girls were too young and Adam's schedule was far from routine. Now that Lucy was in preschool all day three days a week and would be in kindergarten next year, Anna could consider employment.

She sighed as she arranged the chopped fruit and vegetables around a pork roast in the Dutch oven. She poured some apple juice over the meat and veggies and sprinkled on cinnamon, nutmeg and ground cloves. Placing the lid on top, Anna sat the Dutch oven on the range over medium-high heat and began preheating the oven. The thing was that Anna loved the idea of earning money, but not the idea of getting a job she cared nothing about. She had done her fair share of miserable summer jobs through college--retail, secretary in a high profile media company (very stressful!) and even doing reception and payroll in the construction industry! She cared nothing about any of the jobs--never looked back after her last day--it was only about a paycheck. That was okay when Anna was in her teens and early twenties, but she was 33 years old now. She wanted those days to be behind her.

The beeping of the oven let her know that it was preheated and time to put in the rolls. She first brushed the tops with melted butter and then placed the rolls on a baking sheet and slid it in the oven. Adam never pressed her to get a job. She just wanted to take some of the strain off of him, and feel that she was contributing to their debt reduction. But, Anna paused in preparing a peach cobbler, wasn't she still putting others first? Maybe it was some motherhood disease, Anna mused. She felt like she'd lost the ability to think only about herself. She hoped it wasn't degenerative--that there was still time to save herself!

Anna slid the cobbler in the oven. After pouring herself a glass of white wine, she walked to the living room to have a moment of peace while dinner cooked. Adam wasn't yet home, and the girls were downstairs having one of their rare times of happily playing together. Anna guessed Lucy was probably being especially agreeable because Martha had allowed her to play with her very special horses and wooden stable. Anna always treasured these too brief moments when she could at least enjoy the illusion of having the house all to herself. She switched on only two lamps, creating a warm glow. As the sun was setting, Anna closed the blinds and lit a pumpkin scented candle. After turning on the stereo, filling the room with soothing piano music, Anna plopped on her sand colored sectional and picked up her wine

41

glass. One sip later she heard Lucy's feet stomping up the stairs. Anna sighed--Lucy radar strikes again! Somehow that child knew instinctively every time her mother had carved out a moment to herself. Lucy stood before her mother, frowning.

"Mommy, do I have a brain?"

"Of course you do," Anna responded, wondering what had brought all of this on. Before she could ask, Lucy disappeared back downstairs. Curious, she walked over to the top of the stairs to listen.

"Mommy says I do have a brain in my head!" Lucy boasted triumphantly to her sister. Anna heard Martha reply, "Yeah, but how does she know it's really in there? She can't see it." Anna waited to hear what Lucy's response would be. She could almost feel Lucy's frustration, even from where she stood.

"Because, well, God made me!" Lucy finally proclaimed. 'Good answer,' thought Anna. Martha was apparently stumped, because she gave no reply, at least not one that Anna could hear. Grinning, she made her way back to her spot on the couch. Lately Martha had become aware of how gullible her little sister could sometimes be and was having fun exploiting it. The other

42

day Anna heard her telling Lucy that making a 'he's crazy' motion (finger going in circles at the side of the head) really meant that you were very smart. She encouraged Lucy to make that motion any time she met someone. Anna figured Martha should enjoy Lucy's gullible nature while she could. It wouldn't be long before Lucy would be finding her own ways to retaliate!

Anna heard keys jingling outside, and then Adam walked through the front door.

"Hello, dear," he greeted as he sat down his computer bag and lunch sack. He then removed his cell phone from his belt, his ear piece and his pager. Anna often teased him that he was like some bionic superhero, or maybe a Borg in Star Trek, wearing his plethora of electronic gadgets all the time.

"Where are the girls?" he asked, glancing around.

"They're downstairs. They've been playing with Martha's horses."

"Hmmmm."

"So, how was your day?" Anna asked, folding her legs up under her.

"Oh, fine. I had a 100 year old patient today," Adam answered, hanging up his trench coat and cap.

"One hundred years old?!"

"Yeah. She told my nurse that she thought I was such a cute young doctor that she may just get naked before I came back in the room," Anna grinned.

Anna laughed, "That's quite a threat!"

"No kidding...I'm gonna go and get changed. Dinner smells great!"

"Good," Anna said, watching her husband climb the stairs. She was struck, again, by his handsome features. They had been together since high school. They met in chemistry class and worked together on the yearbook. Anna had watched Adam mature from a 16 year old boy to a 32 year old man. She thought he grew more attractive with each year. His dark brown hair was already peppered with gray, which Anna felt gave him an extremely distinguished air. Modern rectangular glasses framed large hazel eyes. His six foot frame seemed taller due to his thin physique. He had a narrow face with a strong Roman-like nose. He wasn't good-looking in a conventional way--he didn't have Ken Barbie-doll looks or those of a jock or movie star. Instead, he was more

44

like the distinguished, handsome college professor that all the young women had a secret crush on.

"Mommy, Mommy," Lucy called, rushing up the steps, "is Daddy home? Did I hear Daddy?"

"Yes, he's gone upstairs to change," Anna explained, getting up from the couch to check on dinner.

"Yeah!" cheered Lucy, racing upstairs to tell her daddy all about her day. Lucy had always kept close tabs on her father. She wanted to know where he was and when he'd be home. She also wanted to keep him up-to-date on all of her doings. Martha loved her dad, too, and enjoyed playing video games with him and discussing anthropology or science. But, she had never kept tabs on him like Lucy did. Anna always wondered if the difference had anything to do with the fact that during Martha's earliest years, Adam was largely absent, and his comings and goings were completely unpredictable. Those days even Anna couldn't keep track of where he was every moment, especially during residency, when he rotated to a different specialty every month. This past year had been quite a switch--he was home every evening and every weekend. Maybe with this newfound routine,

Martha would begin counting on her father's presence a bit more.

Anna could hear Lucy's little voice prattling on upstairs as she walked into the kitchen to see about dinner. She pulled out the sheet of golden rolls and sat it on the trivet on the counter to cool. The cobbler was beginning to bubble nicely, and the roast was at 155 degrees, nearly done. Anna loved living in an area of the country with four distinct seasons. She tried to celebrate the best attributes of each one through food, decorations and family activities. Her absolute favorite season was autumn. In this area of Virginia autumn was often the shortest of all seasons. Summer temperatures often pushed to the end of September, and by Thanksgiving most of the leaves had already fallen. Therefore, the true autumn color was around for only a month or so. Anna made the most of that month by accentuating her living room's autumn tones with her collection of cornhusk wreathes, decorative pumpkins and miniature artificial maple trees. She also made sure the family visited a pumpkin patch and maybe even went apple picking. Lastly, she tried every recipe she could find involving canned pumpkin, and fitted in plenty of what she called

46

'harvest dinners.' Tonight's dinner was one of her favorites. Pairing fall apples with meat and potatoes gave the vegetables a slightly fruity taste and the apples a meaty taste. This time of year she also liked to bake acorn squash, make pumpkin ravioli and delicious pumpkin-nut fudge. She was never sure if her family loved eating it all as much as she loved making it, or if they were just humoring her Either way, she loved fall foods and the family loved her too much to complain.

..... Thirty minutes later the family sat around the dining table together. These family dinners were rare-- usually the girls ate before Adam even got home from work. For them to all eat together each night they'd have to postpone dinner until 7 p.m. or later. Considering the girls went to bed by 8:30, that was pushing it. There were random nights, though, when Anna made a special dinner and Adam was home early. Then they could all eat at the same time. On these occasions Anna lit tapered candles and laid out her only set of china she'd bought when Montgomery Ward went out of business.

After the chaos died down of assembling everyone to the table and filling their plates and glasses, the family was finally ready to eat. Just as Martha picked up her fork, Lucy reminded, "We have to pray!" Lucy attended a church preschool and now took these things quite seriously. Anna didn't mind. She'd been raised attending her grandparents' Baptist church, of which her grandfather was the pastor. She considered herself a Christian, even though she only ushered her family to church intermittently. Adam was open to religion, but hadn't been raised to believe anything in particular. At the moment, Martha was simply annoyed at having to delay eating and being bossed around by her little sister.

"Okay, Lucy, go ahead," Anna encouraged while folding her hands. Adam bowed his head, and Martha put down her fork with a sigh.

"Everybody close your eyes!" ordered Lucy. She tended to be a bit dictatorial with her religious duties. She then began, "God is great, God is--Martha, your eyes are open!"

"Lucy, how would you know if my eyes were open unless yours are, too?!"

"Lucy, just say the prayer before dinner is cold," Adam ordered, with his stomach growling.

"God is great, God is good..um"

48

"Let us thank Him," Anna prompted.

"Right, let us thank Him for our food."

"Amen!" they all said in unison, with Martha and Adam speaking the loudest. They all then eagerly tucked into their harvest dinners.

.... Anna had planned to dive into her grandmother's journal once the girls were in bed. She cleaned up dinner, bathed the girls, and reminded Martha twice to take her asthma medicine and to feed her fish. She then reminded Lucy three times to brush her teeth before reading to her and making sure Martha read a chapter of her required reading. Anna was worn out. Every night was the same-- push, push, push to move both girls through their nighttime routine. She didn't feel she could do her grandmother's writings any justice at that point. Instead, she decided to soak in a hot bath and begin the journal tomorrow, while the girls were at school. One of Anna's favorite features of the townhouse was the master bath. The room was about 8' by 12', with a double sink, standing corner shower and a large garden tub with tile surround and picture window. The bathroom was three stories up, facing the back woods. Therefore, no matter

49

what the season, the view from the window was lovely. Anna could lie back in the tub and gaze at the trees-- sometimes dense with summer foliage, or full of autumn golds and reds. Her favorite was actually in the winter after there had been a snow. It was a marvelous feeling, lying in a steamy, bubbly bath while looking out on a chilly scene of black trunks highlighted by white drifts.

At night Anna liked to leave the bathroom light off and bathe by the glow of a single candle. Tonight she lit a tea scented candle and reclined in the tub, looking at the stars twinkling between the tree branches. She tried to completely empty her mind and just 'be'. It was difficult to maintain, though. Nagging thoughts kept drifting through--'What should I do for dinner tomorrow night?', 'Did Martha remember to put her homework in her backpack?' , 'I need to glance at bills', 'Oh, no! It's time to pay our school loans again!'...Pretty soon her shoulders were up around her ears and her relaxing bath had become anything but.

'Okay,' thought Anna, 'emptying my mind isn't working. I guess I need to fill it, instead.' And, so, her mind began to play with varying scenarios she found

50

relaxing--sitting on the beach, watching the waves; curled up in front of a crackling fire; lying in bed while listening to rain hitting the window panes; comfortably settled on the couch on a Sunday afternoon with a blanket, a sleeping cat and a good book..

"Yes," sighed Anna, "that's better".......

CHAPTER THREE

"Martha, make sure you're eating breakfast! We're leaving in twenty minutes!" called Anna from the kitchen. Martha and Lucy were on the couch, eating breakfast and watching the Smurfs.

"What?!" yelled Lucy.

"Oh, and Martha, check that your homework is in your backpack!" Anna remembered.

"What?!" Lucy yelled again.

"Lucy, I'm not talking to you," Anna said, frustrated.

"Yes you are!" Lucy pointed out.

"Yes, well...I am now, but, oh, never mind!" Anna gave up, exasperated.

Martha turned her head and yelled, "Okay, Mom!"

"You blew bad breath on my banana!" Lucy accused Martha, frowning at her sister and then looking at her banana disgustingly.

No matter how much preparation Anna did the night before, their morning routine was always rushed and harried. She usually laid out their clothes, made lunches and checked their backpacks the night before each school day. She also made Adam's lunch, programmed the coffee maker and had his clothes ironed. Even so, every morning involved feeding the cats, walking the dog, making sure the girls dressed, ate breakfast and brushed their teeth and hair and getting out the door by 7:45. Anna arose by 5:20 each school morning so that she could get a shower, get dressed and at least try to accomplish some sort of beauty routine before the girls arose. In all her years of being a homemaker, she made herself take a shower and apply some make-up each day. She didn't always fuss with her hair--some days it went straight into a clip or ponytail. Other days she actually used the curling iron. Either way, she refused to let herself slip into 'sloppiness'. It was often tempting, but she knew it was crucial to her self-esteem to give some attention to her appearance.

With the Smurf theme music playing on the TV, Anna ushered her girls upstairs to brush their teeth. As she gathered coats, shoes, lunch bags and backpacks, Anna marveled that her girls were watching the Smurfs, just as she had in the '80's. Anna and Faith had owned Smurf figurines and even Smurf sleeping bags. Lots of

53

'80's toy trends had resurfaced--My Little Ponies, Strawberry Shortcake, Care Bears, Holly Hobby, even Weeble-Wobbles and Star Wars! It was sometimes a bit disorienting, like entering a time warp. There were an awful lot of thirty-something adults now kicking themselves for not having saved their toys or kept them in better condition. Adam was still ill at the memory of selling his Star Wars paraphernalia at a garage sale when he was eight. Who knew?! Of course, back then E-Bay didn't even exist.

Anna switched off the television and yelled for the girls to hurry up. She glanced at the gold journal waiting patiently on her desk. "Later," she promised Annie McDowell. She planned to take the girls to school, go to the YMCA and return straight home to devour as much of her grandmother's writings as she could before time to collect Lucy from school. She couldn't wait to get started. She knew it was silly, but somehow she felt the answers to her dissatisfaction and restlessness lay in her grandmother's journal. Anna hadn't even mentioned the journal to Adam last night. It wasn't that it was any great secret. For some reason she just didn't want to share it with anyone until she'd gotten first crack at it.

...... "Are you okay, sweetie? You're kind of quiet this morning," Anna remarked to Martha. They had just dropped off Lucy at preschool and were headed to Martha's school.

"Well, I'm worried about my math quiz today," Martha mumbled.

"Are you having trouble with math?" Anna inquired.

"I'm just not so good at it. I don't understand-- Alexa and Jeffrey are always done before time is up, and they always get everything right! How do they do it?" Martha complained, sounding near tears.

"You get most everything right when I quiz you in the car in the mornings," Anna pointed out, trying to figure out exactly where the problem was.

"Yeah, but the quizzes at school we have to do really fast, 'cause we aren't given much time. Plus, the teacher's using bigger numbers. We have to borrow now for lots of the subtraction problems," Martha said. She began to sound a little calmer as she explained her worries.

"Well, first, try not to worry about Alexa and Jeffrey. Don't compare yourself to them. Do the best you can, okay? Second, we can do more practicing at home--I mean, written, timed quizzes at home," Anna offered.

"'Kay, Momma," Martha agreed, still sounding a bit defeated. There was no time for Anna to console her any further, though, for they had reached Martha's school.

"Bye, dear! You'll do fine!" Anna called after her daughter. Anna sighed as she pointed the car in the direction of the YMCA. She knew how important it was to Martha that she do well in everything. Anna had felt the same drive as a child, and as an adult, too. It didn't really have anything to do with impressing her mother, teacher or classmates. Of course, their praise was welcomed, but the real issue was never letting herself down. Martha had that same motivation. It was both a blessing and a curse, Anna often felt. It meant getting good grades and having doors opened to you; it also meant heavy stress and many sleepless nights. Anna remembered her mother often encouraging her and Faith to take a 'mental health day' in high school. It was just so difficult to take a day off without getting far behind. They were in multiple advanced classes and after school activities, trying to earn their places in a good college. Their hard work paid off, though. They gained early admission to the College of William and Mary, a college known for its high academic standards. And, they had loved every minute of their four undergraduate years. Anna hoped that Martha's drive would prove to be more of a blessing then a curse, and lead her to a career that she was passionate about.

Pulling into the gym parking lot, Anna's thoughts naturally jumped right to her own desire for a career she could feel passionate about. She climbed out of the car and trudged toward the YMCA entrance. The same thoughts began swirling through her head. Ten minutes later pumping on the elliptical machine, she felt as if the cycles of her legs mimicked the cycle of her thoughts. Pump-pump-pump-I don't want to go back to school; pump-pump-pump-I don't want another summer job; pump-pump-pump-I don't want to be completely financially dependent on Adam's career my whole life...Anna felt passionately about what she didn't want. That was no problem! If only she could be as certain about what she did want.

57

Sometimes Anna wondered where her choosiness came from. Lots of people had jobs they didn't feel passionate about, and they got along fine. What was her problem? She often wished she just didn't care. With her education, she could probably get a decent job without too much struggle. Not one she was passionate about, but do-able. Why wasn't that enough? She wondered if her feeling stemmed from having observed her parents over the years.

Anna hobbled off the elliptical machine and headed for the weight section. She was relieved this was a 'leg day.' Anna alternated her strengthening workout-- one day she did all leg weights, the next day was all arm weights. Her leg strength was definitely more impressive than that of her arms, leading her to look forward to 'leg days.' Seated at the hamstring machine, Anna's thoughts returned to her parents' careers. Neither one had finished college, so their choices were a bit more limited. Still, Anna reminded herself with a bitter smile, her B.A. may help get her resume onto the boss's desk, but it hadn't given her any particular skills, either. Moving to the glute machine, Anna pondered her mother's thirty years at the Richmond newspaper. As a divorced woman, she had two girls to provide for. She'd worked as a secretary in the ad department before retiring a year ago. Her mother had never looked back since; in fact, she was thrilled to have 'paid her dues' and be done. Thirty years, five days a week, nine hours a day, only for a paycheck. Her father was the same, except he was still working. Having remarried, with another daughter in college, he didn't have the choice of retiring yet. He'd worked all his life in trucking, first driving and then dispatching from an office. He, too, dreamed of retiring and would never for a moment miss any aspect of the trucking business. Anna understood her parents' need to make a living and provide for a family. She even admired their doggedness and ability to remain loyal to jobs they felt apathetic about. Yet, she didn't understand how millions of people spent the majority of their days and weeks and years in jobs that, at best, they cared nothing about, and at worst, hated every minute of.

Now exercising her calves, Anna pondered herself a moment. She figured that, unconsciously, she had always been determined to have more than just a paycheck. She had never wanted to live like her parents, and countless others. 'Jobs' were okay to get started, but

59

she wanted to spend her life enjoying a career, if not rejoicing in a calling. She believed her parents had callings, too, but had never followed them. Her father had amazing artistic talents--charcoals, pencil and ink drawings, and even whittling sculptures from wood. He'd had no real training, but his work looked truly professional. He also was a born entrepreneur. At the mention of any business venture, he would immediately begin working out all the numbers in his head of how to get it off the ground. Her mother, also, had God-given gifts that Anna felt had never been truly realized. Anna's mother would have made an excellent professor or author in something like history or theology. She was actually pursuing a teaching degree before she left college to get married. Ever since Anna could remember, her mother had devoured books and written volumes of her own in terms of diaries and lengthy e-mails to friends. Yet, neither parent had truly pursued their passions, or found a way to make a living from them. Anna sighed as she headed for the mats to do her stretches. Usually she enjoyed this last workout ritual--rewarding her tired muscles with long, drawn-out stretches that felt so good. Today, though, she felt as if she were only going through the motions. Her career thoughts had led her back to the same spot--guilt. Who was she to criticize her parents, or anyone else who was making a living and supporting themselves? She certainly had never done even that much. She went from living at home to living in dorms, and then living off of school loans, to finally living off Adam's salary. It was well and good to be determined to follow one's passion when someone else was paying the bills! Feeling disgusted with herself and as dissatisfied as ever, Anna grabbed her purse and sweatshirt from the locker room and simply left the gym.

"Oh, what the heck," she muttered to herself as she turned into the Burger King drive thru on the way home. She didn't usually get food after working out, or, if she did, she tried to choose something a little healthier. However, feeling down and self-indulgent, Anna hurried home with her bacon biscuit and hash browns in an attitude of defiance.

....   Anna walked Max, their beagle/basset mix, quickly around the townhouse complex (or, as quickly as his squatty legs could travel). She then settled down on the couch with her sinful brunch. She devoured every last

61

crumb while watching 'The Ellen DeGeneres Show' and then went upstairs to take a hot shower and wash away the grease. Once Anna was out of the shower and dressed, the phone rang. Checking caller id, she answered, "Hi, Faith! How's it going?"

"Nod so gread. I've god a cold."

"Oh, I'm sorry, sweetie. I guess we are entering cold season." She wasn't surprised Faith was sick. She was seven months pregnant and worked with young kids all day as a speech therapist. She was entering that phase of pregnancy when one is tired and heavy feeling and her defenses were down. "Otherwise, are you and the baby okay?"

"Yeah, we're fide. I decided to cancel some of my kids today, so I can rest." Just then Faith had a tremendous coughing fit, preventing Anna from responding. Once the coughing subsided, Faith said, "Oh, crap. I peed sombe in my pants."

"Oh, I'm sorry, dear," Anna said, lovingly amused. How she remembered those third trimester moments of heartburn, incontinence and swollen feet. And they say pregnant women are supposed to be glowing and beautiful!

62

"I'm nod sure if I hab any clead maternity pands I habn't peed in," Faith said, sounding defeated. "I guess I should go and look. I'll talk to you later."

"Alright. Call me if you need me, okay? I love you!"

"Lob you! Bye!"

.... After what seemed like days, Anna was finally seated on the couch with a fragrant cup of coffee and her grandmother's golden journal. She figured she had maybe two hours before she needed to walk Max again and drive back to Lucy's school. "Okay, Granny, what do you have to tell me?" Anna actually asked aloud as she slowly opened the journal to the first entry.

March 8, 1955

Beginning a new journal--I hope it's one of many new beginnings for me. I'm trying, God, to get back on track with myself by first getting reconnected with You. Please bless these morning times together so that I can get close with You again. I'm a little lost on exactly how to go about it.

When I reread my journal from the past four years or so, I was devastated.

63

"Where is that journal?" Anna wondered.

All through it were the same themes, the same ups and downs. The main dissatisfactions involved my weight and lack of direction in my life.

'I didn't know Granny ever had a weight problem. I wonder what she means by 'direction'?'

I've finally realized that what I first need to do is reconnect with Spirit. So, I'm trying to make changes in my life. I want to capture the relationship I once had with You. How do I begin?......

.... Annie, I've been here all those years of your ups and downs, waiting for you to return to Me.

'What is Granny doing?! It's her handwriting--it looks like she's writing to herself! She's writing what God would potentially tell her.'

There is no secret in how to find Me again--I'm already there with you now. You only need to open your heart and mind to Me again. You need to stop fighting and struggling. Surrender your anger, frustration and fatigue and let Me help you. I want to help. I've been eagerly waiting to step in and give you peace, as well as all your dreams and even more. Change and relief do not have to be months and years in the coming. You will feel better

64

*even today! You wouldn't believe where your life could
be a year from now! I have great goals for all of your
gifts that are waiting to be started. Today, dream of all
that you want and simply look and listen for Me. Don't
forget that your main purpose in living is to grow
spiritually. Spiritual strength leads to a much fulfilled
life.*

Anna finished reading the first entry and paused
to sip her coffee. So, her grandmother, also, struggled
with her weight. Somehow, at some point, she must have
conquered it, because Anna had only ever known her
grandmother as a petite little thing. Apparently Annie
McDowell also struggled with some sort of lack of
direction. That bit surprised Anna even more. Annie,
like most women in the '50's, was a housewife. Though
she never wanted to admit it to anyone, Anna had actually
envied women of that generation. Their choices were
more limited, of course, but it also simplified things a bit.
The term 'stay-at-home-mother' didn't even exist.
Mothers simply did that--remained at home and took care
of their family. Even if they weren't always satisfied in
that role, at least it was approved of and respected.
Although Anna certainly supported the idea of the

65

feminist movement, it had made things confused for her generation. Women seemed to have to defend any position they took--staying at home or going to work, and many ran themselves ragged doing all of it. It was a damned-if-you-do/damned-if-you-don't situation.

Anna had always felt there were a lot of mixed messages out there for mothers these days. On one hand, there were definitely still remnants of the feminist movement. Women in positions of power and earning their own living were highly admired. Girls were now encouraged more than ever to enter into the up and coming careers of science and technology, or become the first woman president. There was certainly a stigma attached to the word 'housewife'. On the other hand, there has been a push for women to return to the home. There has been a reawakening to the importance of mothers raising and directly influencing their children, especially in their formative years. Home schooling has gained popularity. Mother's groups have formed across the country. There has been a return to the domestic arts led by such icons as Martha Stewart. However, there's also the popular term 'soccer mom,' not meant to be flattering.

It connotes an upper middle class mom driving a minivan, 'playing' mother and looking stylish about it.

So, when Anna told someone she just met that she was a stay-at-home mother, she honestly never knew how they would react. She'd read everything in their faces from admiration to boredom to ridicule. Of course, if she were truly proud and satisfied in her role, then it wouldn't matter how anyone else reacted. Perhaps she was too insecure or needful of other's approval. It was just that at Adam's office get-togethers, full of doctors and their professional spouses, her end of the conversation tended to dwindle as people shared 'what they did.' She could see their eyes glaze over at the first mention of potty training or Girl Scouts. Not wanting to be one of those tiring mothers who can only discuss their children, Anna often said next to nothing. That was what bothered her so deeply--if she subtracted her husband and her children out of the equation of her life, there was nothing left. Who was *Anna,* separate from the identity of wife of Adam and mother of Martha and Lucy? It was a most disturbing void.

Before Anna could move on to the second entry in the journal, the phone rang. Glancing at the caller id, Anna answered, "Hey there, Barbara!"

"I don't know if I'll ever get used to people knowing it's me even before they answer!" Barbara said.

"Yeah, I know. Even with caller id, I forget others are using it, too," Anna admitted.

"It sure takes the fun out of prank calls, not that I ever did those."

"No, of course not," Anna teased.

"So, what was I calling about, anyway?" Barbara wondered aloud. Anna chuckled. She and Barbara had an uncanny knack for spending an endless amount of time talking about anything and everything--except the main point of the call.

"Oh yeah, are you still able to meet on Friday?" Barbara remembered.

"Yeah, sure. How about we meet at the coffee shop around 11 a.m.? That'll give me time to work out and change."

"Okay, sounds good."

"Do you mind if I invite Charlotte, too? She may be able to leave the kids with her neighbor for a couple of hours." Barbara and Charlotte had met a few times, but for some reason Anna generally hung out with one or the other. Anna had an idea forming and thought she'd like both of her friends in on it.

"Sure," Barbara said, "the more the merrier!"

"Great, I'll call her and see if she can line up a sitter. See ya Friday!"

"Bye!"

Anna decided to call Charlotte later. She knew if she got her on the phone now she'd lose the last precious hour she had to herself. She loved Charlotte dearly, but she was one of those people who simply could not have a brief phone conversation. No matter how many times and ways you found to say 'I guess I'll go now', Charlotte could stretch even the farewell to fifteen minutes or more. Instead, Anna turned back to her grandmother's journal to continue reading.

March 9, 1955

I think overall that I really did have a better day yesterday for having put in this morning time. One thing really struck me about the writings in my old journal. Once I got over feeling down that nothing in my life had changed I noticed something--all I did in all that writing

69

was complain, complain, complain. I'm tired of complaining. I want change instead. Help me to make better choices in my life so these cycles will end. When I do slip, Spirit, help me to forgive myself and carry on rather than using that as an excuse to go back to old habits.

I also need to remember gratitude and fit that into my everyday life as well. I forget to thank You, Spirit. You have blessed me with more than I can begin to list. Help me to begin noticing and remembering to thank You more often for all of it. I want to get back to when I did notice all the little special things of life and took great pleasure and fulfillment in them.

.... Annie, you're doing the most important thing you can right now by deciding that you want your life to change and being open to it. You've wanted change for so long, but you haven't really wanted it enough to let Me in and give up what have become angry and self-defeating habits. The more you complain about a thing, the more of it you bring into your life, because that's all you're thinking about. You first have to change what you're always thinking and talking about if you want real change in your life. So, yes, stop complaining about what you

70

don't want and begin talking about what you do want. And, yes, a crucial first step is to be truly grateful for all you already have. I love to give more blessings to those who notice and appreciate them. I want it all for you, Annie, all that you have and all you've dreamed of. It's all right there at your fingertips. You just need to decide that you're ready for life again. You know that you've been only existing these last few years, even afraid of truly living. Well, it's time to live again, don't you think?.....

...... You're right. I have been afraid to live, afraid to give You the reins of my life. It makes me think of women getting make-overs--you know, surrendering themselves to beauticians and seeing the results. Often they're nervous because even if they don't currently like themselves, they're used to their look and it's safe and familiar. Will they like their new look? Will others? Will they like the new attention they're gaining by looking so great? I think that's how I've been feeling. I've been scared to allow You to give my life a make-over. What would I think of the new me? Would it be too scary, too unrecognizable, too hard to maintain, too wonderful? I'm still a little nervous, but I'm ready to surrender myself

71

and my life to Your sculpting hands. I want to be virtually
unrecognizable to myself and others in the most glorious
way.

Anna set the journal down and simply said,
"Wow." She needed a minute to mull over what she'd
read. Her instincts had been right, though. "This journal
does have a lot to teach me." Anna reached for her coffee
cup, but the coffee had gone cold. She simply set the cup
back down and stared out the window, thinking. What
had she done all morning?--complain, at least in her head,
about all she didn't want. In fact, that's pretty much what
she'd been doing these past three months to anyone and
everyone who would listen. Her case alone seemed to
prove the journal right--all her complaining had only
resulted in more to complain about. What would happen
if she were to shift her focus from what she didn't want to
what she did want? The possibilities made her heart skip
a beat, in excitement and anxiety. Her grandmother had
been right--make-overs could be scary. The easy, though
not satisfying, thing for Anna to do would be to continue
to stay 30 pounds overweight, find some boring office job
to fill her time, and continue moaning about all of it. The
risky, though fulfilling thing for her to do would be to

72

stop complaining--become fit and sexy and to go after a passion of hers, making it into a career.

As Anna snapped Max's leash on and headed out the door, her thoughts turned to another issue raised in the journal, gratitude. As she walked along the sidewalk, she decided to challenge herself--for every townhouse she passed, she'd list one of her blessings. Considering the townhouses were stacked side-by-side for blocks, she wasn't really sure she could do it. Still, she began...Adam, Martha, Lucy, their home, their health, two working cars, this free day of Anna's, Adam's job, their pets, food in the house, heat, electricity, water, plenty of clothes and shoes, extended family, books to read, health insurance, coats, toys, their educations...Anna found that the more things she listed, the more good things came into her head. By the time she'd circled back to her townhouse, she still had more items to list. As she unhooked Max's leash and let him go drink, she realized she had a goofy grin on her face. She felt her heart was bursting. "How in the world could I have been feeling sorry for myself earlier this morning?" Heading out the door to pick up Lucy, Anna felt she was walking on air.

73

....   "So, how was your school day?" Anna asked
Lucy while driving home, "Did you work on your letters
and numbers?"

        "Katie had a rock up her nose," Lucy said.

        "A rock?!" Anna exclaimed.

        "Just a little rock," Lucy clarified.

        "So, what happened?"

        "She blowed it out," Lucy explained.

        "Oh, good," Anna said. Glancing in her rearview
mirror, she noticed Lucy holding a tiny stuffed bear.
"Where did your bear come from?"

        "From the red box," Lucy answered.

        "What red box?" Anna inquired.

        "The one in my class," Lucy responded,
beginning to get annoyed with her mother.

        "Is it the prize box?" Anna asked, desperately
trying to solve this simple mystery.

        "Yeah," Lucy answered shortly.

        "That's great! Why did you go to the prize box?"

        "'Cause Mrs. Chase told me to," Lucy said, fully
exasperated by her mother's lack of understanding.

"But why did she send you to the prize box?" Anna asked, sorry she'd ever brought up the subject of the bear.

"BECAUSE SHE'S THE TEACHER!" Lucy practically shouted.

"Okay okay, Lucy," Anna sighed with a tired smile. She could never get a clear picture of Lucy's preschool day from Lucy herself. It was like trying to break some obscure code every Monday, Wednesday and Friday. All she'd learned today was that Katie had blown a rock out of her nose and Lucy had received a prize for some reason. Well, that was more than she learned some days!

Not wishing to venture into another discussion with Lucy, Anna spent the rest of the drive home enjoying the fall foliage. Thanksgiving was rushing at them with alarming speed. Then there would be all of the Christmas hoop-la! Anna didn't even want to begin thinking along that line. "Live in the moment," she reminded herself. And, this moment was definitely not about Christmas chaos! Instead, she began planning what she'd fix for dinner. Maybe another favorite fall feast!

.... Later that evening, Anna was busy making her fall dinner while Martha worked on her homework.

"How did your math quiz go today?" Anna asked lightly. She'd been concerned about Martha all afternoon, but she'd waited to see if her daughter would volunteer any information herself. She'd been quiet ever since she stepped off the bus. It's funny, Anna mused, we grow up thinking our moms are practically psychic, that they have some supernatural ability to see into our lives and minds and know everything. In reality, it's just that kids' emotions show plainly on their faces and in their body language, no matter how well they think they're hiding them.

"I didn't finish all the problems in time, again," Martha confessed with slumped shoulders. "I know how to do the problems; I'm just not fast enough!"

"When is your next timed test?" Anna asked.

"Next Wednesday," Martha replied, already dreading the event.

"Well, this weekend we'll do several practice tests at home, all timed. All you need to do is build your confidence," Anna reassured her.

"Alright," Martha mumbled, not convinced. Trying to lighten the mood, Anna said, "Tomorrow's supposed to be a little warmer and sunny. If you finish your homework today, you could play outside with Ellen after school." Ellen lived just two doors up from Martha. She was a year younger than Martha, but the two had become fast friends as soon as they'd moved to the townhouse complex.

"Yay," Martha said, her eyes lighting up. "We want to start our Nature Club!"

"Nature club?" Anna asked. This was the first she'd heard of the friends' newest project. Both Ellen and Martha shared the same passion, wildlife. It was a bond that could not be broken.

"Yeah, we decided to start a Nature Club, and anyone who's nice to animals and doesn't kill bugs can join," Martha explained excitedly.

"Well, that sounds like fun. Can Lucy join, too?" She could already see that this club might cause difficulties. Lucy never wanted to be excluded from anything her older sister did. As usual, though, Martha proved to be generously forgiving. With a sigh, she answered, "I guess so, if she follows the rules."

"That's sweet of you," Anna said, relieved. While Martha finished her spelling and word problem worksheet, Anna concentrated on finishing her dinner preparations. She'd decided on ravioli with pumpkin sauce. It was such an easy, quick meal to fix. She simply bought the frozen ravioli, meat or cheese filled, and made a pumpkin sauce to pour over it, in lieu of alfredo or marinara. The pumpkin sauce consisted of canned pumpkin, chicken broth, heavy cream and a dash of cinnamon and nutmeg. She liked to toast chopped pecans and sprinkle them on top. Served with a fall vegetable such as acorn squash and cider to drink, the meal was a favorite fall standby.

.... Anna found herself ushering the family through dinner and the girls through bath time rather distractedly. She wanted to get the girls in bed so that she could read more of the journal. Once both little bodies had been tucked in and each little head was kissed goodnight, Anna changed into her favorite sweatshirt and drawstring pants. With a mug of hot milk and honey on her bedside table, she propped up the pillows and sat back with the gold journal. About that moment Adam come in to find his

78

favorite Brooklyn hooded sweatshirt. He loved the hoodie his sisters had bought him in New York, despite the fact that when he first put it on, unshaven, Lucy said he looked like a bad guy.

"What's that you're reading?" he asked, pulling on the sweatshirt.

"It's my granny Annie McDowell's journal. I found it the other day when I was going through the storage room.

"Have you read any of it?"

"Yeah, I read some this morning. It's really wonderful. I think it's got a lot of good advice in it," Anna said, unable to suppress her excitement.

"Is that why you've seemed different tonight?"

"What do you mean, different?"

"I don't know, kind-of happy, I guess," Adam said stumbling, trying to find the right words. Anna's first reaction was to be defensive, as if Adam were implying she wasn't generally pleasant to be around. She paused before making some snappy remark, though. If she were absolutely honest with herself, she hadn't been much fun for quite a long time. Literally for years Anna had been at least mildly depressed. Ever since quitting graduate

79

school to stay home with Martha, she had felt lost, and perhaps a bit of a failure.

"I'm sorry, Adam."

"Why?" he asked, completely confused.

"I know I've been difficult to live with," Anna admitted.

"Anna, I didn't mean that--" Adam began.

"I know," Anna interrupted, "but it's true. I haven't been happy, I mean really happy, for so long. I'm tired of it. I'm not sure where I'm going next, but I want things to be different."

"That's great, Anna," Adam said gently, sitting on the bed beside her. "And all of that is from reading the journal?"

"Yeah, sort-of. It's just helping me realize I've been looking at everything all wrong. I think I've unknowingly been keeping myself down all these years. I mean, I've been blaming all the circumstances around me for my unhappiness, and telling anyone who'll listen. And all it's done is made me very aware of how dissatisfied I am. I'm just starting to wonder what would happen if I did the opposite," Anna paused for a moment. "What would happen if I only focused on what makes me happy,

80

and only talked about all the blessings I have and all the good that I want out of life?"

Adam smiled, "It would be a worthwhile experiment."

"Yes, it would."

Adam leaned over and kissed her before saying, "Well, I'll let you get to your reading. Keep me informed!"

After Adam left the room, Anna sipped her hot milk and opened to the next entry.

April 2, 1955

Lately I've wanted to incorporate more creativity into my life. I have been doing some needlepoint, but that alone doesn't seem to be enough. I've always loved decorating. I think I've done about all I can with my own home, though, short of major remodeling that we can't afford. The other day my friend, Janet, said something about how lovely my home was and how she wished someone would come in and redo her house for her. She may have been joking, but it got me thinking. Wouldn't it be something if I were to do that for other people?

'Funny,' thought Anna, 'I did that exact thing for a year or two.' She'd actually considered starting her own

81

decorating business once the girls were older. But, difficult clients always changing their minds and nit-picking her work had made her reconsider. 'You may not know what you're getting into, Granny!' Anna mentally warned. *I guess I could charge money for that sort of thing! But, I don't have any training. I'd have no idea what to charge. Besides, would people actually want to pay me? I think I'd be too scared to go into other peoples' homes and make changes. I mean, what if they hated it? I'd be mortified! Anyway, please give me guidance....*

.... *Being creative is one of the spiritual gifts I've given you. I intend for you to use it. Creativity comes in many forms, cooking, painting, gardening, writing...You're already practicing creativity in many ways every day, you just haven't been acknowledging or noticing all that is creative in your day-to-day doings. Try to notice it today; take pleasure in all the things you create and gain pride and energy from them. You need to stop listing all of your supposed limitations and fears and instead, use that same imagination to think of all the wonderful possibilities for you. I gave you imagination and the power of thought for a reason. You can use it to create your dreams. If you can imagine it and believe in*

82

it, you can have it. Your thoughts have great power
behind them, so use them to your advantage. Think of all
you want, all you'd love to see unfold in your life.
Imagine it until you can believe in it, and it will come
true.

Anna went to bed that night with those words on her mind. 'Imagine it, imagine it, until you can believe in it, and it will come true!'

CHAPTER FOUR

"So, does Chris have his mohawk yet?" Anna asked Barbara, grinning.

Rolling her eyes, Barbara answered, "He's got a hair appointment next week. Can you imagine?! Why did I ever start this bet?" Charlotte looked from one woman to the other, bewildered. Anna explained about the challenge to raise Chris's grades.

"Well, are his grades any better?" Charlotte inquired.

"Actually, yes, and so far they seem to be staying good," Barbara said, pleased.

"Well, then it's only hair. Hairdos are temporary, but grades are permanent!" Charlotte summed up. Barbara smiled gratefully at her. The two were still getting to know one another. Anna could tell they were going to get along famously in no time.

A comfortable silence settled in as the three women sipped their coffee. Barbara had arrived at the coffee shop first, managing to claim one of the coveted tables by the gas log fireplace. Anna had shown up soon after and ordered a cup of coffee and a bagel before gratefully cozying up to the fire. Lastly Charlotte had blown in the door, looking as hurried and flustered as ever with a bright smile on her face. With all of their respective children safely deposited at school or with a babysitter, the women could enjoy a rare bit of quiet calm and adult conversation. Only full-time mothers can appreciate how truly sacred and reverent such a moment is.

"So," Barbara said, finally breaking the silence, "how is your basement cleaning out project going?"

"Well, actually," Anna said, somehow nervous all the sudden, "that's part of the reason I wanted to meet with you both." She was aware of her friends' questioning stares as she continued. After explaining how she came to find the journal, she explained. "There are some really neat ideas in my grandmother's writings." She didn't want her friends to dismiss her grandmother as half loony. "And, I thought maybe we could put some of her ideas to a test," Anna finished a bit weakly. Barbara and Charlotte looked at each other and then back at Anna.

"What kind of ideas?" Barbara asked.

"What kind of test?" Charlotte wondered.

"See, for a long time I haven't been really happy, really satisfied with my life. Nothing's been truly wrong, but I haven't been fulfilled. I mean, more often than not I see a day as just a routine to get through, if not a struggle. Making lunches, fixing dinner, doing laundry, getting groceries, walking the dog--none of it's bad, but not great, either." Anna paused to sip her coffee, wondering if her friends understood what she was trying to say. "It's like I've been existing more than living. And any time I thought of making a real change, like dieting or taking classes in something or making money of my own, I always pointed to all these circumstances and limitations that kept me right where I was. Well, I'm beginning to think maybe I've been my own worst enemy all along...Is any of this making any sense?" Anna finally asked directly. She had no idea what her friends were thinking in that moment.

After what seemed to Anna like an eternity, Barbara asked, "Yeah, I think I do know what you mean. But, isn't that just life?"

"Well, yes and no. That's what I mean. Yes, doing the laundry and getting groceries are part of life, but they shouldn't be all that life is...and," Anna said

86

thoughtfully, "maybe there's even a way to make chores more enjoyable."

"Whistle while you work?" Charlotte joked, and then immediately apologized, "I'm sorry, Anna, I just don't quite get what you're talking about."

Refusing to give up, Anna pressed on, "I think the key is to begin right where you are. My grandmother wrote about the importance of gratitude--really noticing and appreciating all that you have right now. You know, once I began consciously listing all the good things in my life, I was almost overwhelmed. I went from feeling sorry for myself to feeling like the richest woman on earth in the course of a few minutes!" Anna smiled at her friends triumphantly. They continued to look at her skeptically, but with a hint of interest now in their eyes.

"See, once I realized I could consciously change my attitude, my outlook, my feelings, it was like I wasn't a victim anymore. Instead of feeling knocked down by circumstances, I could be the one in control," Anna paused for a moment. "I felt like I had to share it with other people. I thought maybe we could all three try it and let each other know how it changes things."

"Try what, exactly?" Barbara asked.

"Try practicing gratitude," Anna said. "I've heard both of you say similar things as me--that oftentimes life is mostly ho-hum, same ol', same ol'. What if it could be glorious and full of joy?"

"Okay," Charlotte agreed, "I'm game! What do I do?" Anna smiled gratefully at her friend. Charlotte could always be counted on to be a team player, the cheerleader in the crowd. She also tended to look at life philosophically, so this little 'mind' experiment interested her.

Barbara, on the other hand, still looked reluctant. She was more of a grounded, I'll-believe-it-when-I-see-it type of person. But, she loved her friend, Anna, and she felt honored that Anna had wanted to include her in what was obviously a personal journey. So, reserving her skepticism, she said, "Alright, I'll try, too."

"Great!" Anna said, relieved. "I didn't really have anything in particular in mind. I mean, the journal didn't lay out a seven step process or anything. What if we just agree for the next few days to notice things that make our lives happier or easier? We could either write them down or just sort-of keep a mental log. Then, we could meet again and compare how it worked."

"I think I could get my neighbor to baby-sit again next Friday. She's off on Fridays. What if we meet in a week?" Charlotte suggested.

"Sounds good to me," Anna agreed. Both friends looked at Barbara.

"Is this peer pressure?" she asked with a smile. "Okay, okay, I'll be there." Heading out to her car, though, Barbara wondered what she'd got herself into.

.... In the days following the friends' meeting, Anna kept realizing that she was forgetting to remember gratitude. It was just so easy to travel through the day on automatic pilot. 'I can't go back next week with nothing to report, after I started this whole thing!' Anna thought to herself. So, she decided to try using a reminder. Because she rarely wore bracelets, she chose to sport a chunky beaded bracelet on her right wrist, where she couldn't fail to notice it repeatedly. She vowed that each time she became aware of the bracelet, she'd take a second to be grateful for something specific. The first day it nearly drove her crazy. The bracelet seemed to be jingling at her constantly. It certainly did drill the reminder in her head, though, and what surprised her was that she was never at a loss for something to be grateful about. Sometimes it was something as tiny as getting a shopping cart with all four wheels working right or hearing a song on the radio she liked, but there was always something. Still, as Anna got ready for bed that night, she said, "I'm grateful to be taking this damn bracelet off!"

The talisman worked, though. The next day Anna left the bracelet in her jewelry box, and she still found herself remembering gratitude much more frequently. By the third day, to keep things from getting too repetitive, she decided to divide up the remainder of the week into themes. She thought she'd spend one day remembering to be grateful for her home, one day all about her kids, one day about Adam, one about all her personal 'yummies' and one about things outside her home. During her 'grateful for my home' day, Anna went through her normal routine and housework, but it didn't seem quite so monotonous, and even felt a little special here and there. She noticed how cozy the living and kitchen areas were early in the morning when the sky was just beginning to lighten and the coffee was perking. She felt she was in a softener sheet commercial as she inhaled the warm, clean smell of fresh laundry as she folded clothes from the dryer. (Then she realized she'd left a large lipstick stain on the towel she was smelling and had to throw it back in the washer.) She even rearranged a few framed photos and figurines while dusting, just for a difference.

During Anna's 'grateful for my kids day' she tried to slow down and truly engage each girl rather than bustle around them. It broke her heart to see how readily Martha, in particular, responded to and blossomed in her mother's attention. Anna felt that Martha probably got taken for granted oftentimes, because she was always so responsible and well behaved. Lucy, being younger and having the personality of a tiny pre-Madonna, demanded so much more attention--not always in a good way, but attention nonetheless. Anna found that after simply hugging Martha more, asking her more detailed questions about school and friends and truly listening, Martha's shell opened. She was animated, talkative, and by the end of the day, stuck to Anna's side right up 'till bedtime. As Anna pulled Martha's blankets up to her chin, she sat beside her on the bed a moment.

A little nervously Anna said, "I think our practice math quizzes at home have helped, don't you?"

Martha nodded. "Well, I think there's something else that could help, maybe even more." Seeing she had Martha's attention, Anna plunged forward. "Your attitude about your math ability has a lot to do with your quiz scores. See, if you don't believe you're any good at math, then you won't be. On the other hand, if you believe you can do well, then you will."

"Really?" Martha asked hopefully. Anna prayed she wasn't leading her daughter wrong as she answered, "Yeah, it's really very simple. So, just start trying to change your attitude about math and see how it helps."

"Okay, Momma." Anna bent down and kissed Martha's forehead before switching off the light and walking next door to Lucy's room.

When Anna was tucking Lucy in, she said lovingly, "I wanna be just like you when I grow up, Mommy."

"Oh, how sweet, dear," Anna smiled gently, thinking that's just what every mother wants to hear. "How do you want to be like Mommy?"

"I wanna be short."

"Oh," Anna said, her smile faltering a little.

"Yeah, I don't ever wanna be taller than you, Mommy, 'cause then it would be hard to hug you."

"Oh, Lucy, we'll always have no trouble sharing hugs, no matter how much you grow."

"Maybe if I grow really tall," Lucy said brightly, "I could hold you!"

"Um, yeah...well, good night, sweetie."

.... As she did with her girls, on her 'grateful for Adam day' Anna simply gave her husband a bit more of her undivided attention. It amazed her how shifting the focus off of herself not only benefited her family, but Anna, as well. She found that she had more energy and her day felt more purposeful, fuller. And it wasn't as if she were making any drastic changes. For Adam, she simply took a little more care to pack him a lunch he'd enjoy. In the morning she took a few moments to chat with him while he shaved. As he left for work, Anna gave him a hug and a true kiss--to which he responded most readily, leaving her flushed as she went to find breakfast for the girls.

"Are you sick, Momma?" Lucy asked.

"No, why?"

"'Cause your face is pink. I think maybe you have a temp-ter!"

That evening Adam ate two helpings of one of his favorite dinners, a bowl layered with buttery mashed potatoes, beneath salt and pepper cabbage, beneath browned smoked sausage, accompanied by a dark beer. Of course, hours later he had a prolonged bathroom visit. He emerged from the bathroom asking sheepishly, "Do we own a plunger?"

"I'm not sure," Anna grinned, "we may have gotten rid of it in our last move. It was pretty old."

With a sigh, Adam said, "I've got to go out and buy a plunger." He paused while gathering his wallet and keys. "Is there anything else we need?"

"I don't think so."

"I've got to buy something else," Adam said looking embarrassed and amused, "I can't stand in line with only a plunger."

Anna laughed, "Well, you should do it up right-- get a plunger and a box of laxatives."

Adam chuckled, "Yeah, and a box of flushable wipes!" Soon the two of them were laughing helplessly. As Adam headed out the door, Anna sat wiping her tearing eyes. She thought, 'I'm so grateful that after more than a decade of marriage, Adam and I can still make each other laugh.'

Anna really enjoyed her 'grateful for personal yummies day.' She brewed some of her favorite chocolate flavored coffee to begin her day, rendering it nearly sinful with the addition of chocolate mint creamer. After getting the girls to school and wearing herself out at the gym, Anna returned home for an unprecedented midday bath. Both cats and the dog were peering at her curiously as she settled in the steaming tub. After a nice long soak, Anna put on her most comfy jeans and favorite sweater--a coral colored Eddie Bauer v-neck. She then settled on the couch with a decorating magazine, a store-bought salad and her favorite soap opera. Of course, two bites into her salad, the phone rang.

"Hi, Faith," Anna said after swallowing. "How are ya?"

"I'm doing fine. My cold's gone."

"Good! And how's little one?"

"He's doin' great, kicking my ribs and sitting on my bladder. I think I'm gonna have to go shopping soon. I have one pair of shoes that still fit, and I feel like my clown feet are about to burst out of those, too. Anyway, how have you been?"

"Well, I found Granny's journal among a bunch of our papers, and I've been reading it. I know it sounds weird, but it's been helping me to change my outlook on life. I even have Charlotte and Barbara in on it."

"How are they in on it?"

"Well, right now we're all trying to be more aware of our blessings. You know, appreciating all the good things in our lives. It's been really changing how I feel about things."

"Sounds interesting. Let me know how it goes. I might want to join in!"

"Sure!"

"Look, I better go. I have to pee again!"

"Bye," laughed Anna.

That evening Anna continued to celebrate her favorite yummies by lighting a new Yankee 'Butter cream' candle (which, unfortunately, had the family thinking she was baking a dessert). She also put on her most wonderful pajamas as soon as the sun set--you know, the ones that are so comfortably forgiving, thin and soft that it's a miracle they don't fall apart in your hands. She

96

ended her day by curling up on the bed with a delicious
new mystery she'd found at the library and read until her
eyelids could no longer lift their own weight.

Anna's 'grateful for things outside of my home
day' naturally involved spending at least part of the day
out. After getting Martha safely on the bus, Anna and
Lucy headed out to the bookstore. Anna adored
bookstores--the quiet, the unhurried search for that gem of
a book among thousands of potential ones, the soothing
background music and oftentimes the smell of brewing
coffee. She and Lucy first settled at a cafe table with hot
drinks. Lucy licked the whipped cream from the top of
her hot chocolate while Anna sipped her cafe mocha.

"So, how's your day, Mommy?" Anna smiled at
the large blue eyes gazing up at her. Lucy often tried to
play the role of Anna's grown up confidante in settings
such as this. Anna played along.

"I'm having a fine day. And yourself?"

"What?"

"How's your day going?"

"Oh, it's good...I think maybe I'll get a chapter
book today."

97

"Really?" Lucy wasn't even reading yet, but she always saw her sister and mother picking up their latest novels with relish.

"Yeah," Lucy said, sipping her drink and leaving a hot chocolate mustache on her lip. "What are you gonna get?"

"I'm not sure," Anna said thoughtfully, "I'd like to look at the magazines. There should be a lot of good ones about Thanksgiving recipes....you know, Thanksgiving is only a week away!"

"Is that why you're happy?"

"What?" Anna was a bit taken aback.

"Are you happy about Thanksgiving? You've been smiling a lot."

'Well, well,' thought Anna, 'out of the mouths of babes...' This gratitude thing must be working. So far two of the three family members had commented on her elevated mood. Of course, it also left her pondering for a moment what a drag she must have been to live with only last week.

"I am excited about Thanksgiving. I'm also just happy in general." When Lucy looked at her mother questioningly, Anna pressed on. "Aren't you ever happy

98

just because? You know, 'cause of all the good things God's given you, like your family---"

"And my Barbies!"

"Right, and plenty of good food to eat--"

"And my Polly Pocket dolls!"

"Yes, and warm clothes---"

"And tons of My Little Ponies!"

'Hm,' thought Anna, 'we seem to have our priorities a bit skewed here.' But, she didn't want to ruin the moment by preaching to her daughter. So, instead, she agreed, "'Yes, well, sometimes remembering all the good things in my life makes me happy."

"Me, too! I'm happy too!" Lucy beamed.

Thirty minutes later the happy pair left, Anna with a British Country Living Magazine and Lucy clutching her 'chapter book,' a collection of Disney Princess stories. They drove over to a nearby man-made pond. It was encircled by sidewalks and benches and was home to a surprisingly large collection of ducks and geese. Because the day was unseasonably warm and sunny, Anna thought Lucy would enjoy some outdoor time. Ten minutes later, though, when they were being accosted by huge honking geese and Lucy climbed

99

practically on top of her head, Anna reconsidered. Stumbling over to a bench, trying to hold Lucy high and circumvent the aggressive geese, Anna had an attack of the giggles. She finally plunked them both down on the wooden seat, wiping her streaming eyes and reassuring Lucy, "It's okay, sweetie, they'll leave us alone in a minute." Sure enough, once the geese and ducks realized the newcomers had brought no goodies, they slowly disbursed, returning to their little duck and goose agendas. Anna and Lucy sat contentedly, enjoying the thin warmth of the November sun and gazing at the smattering of bobbing ducks, like corks, in the pond. Anna mentally listed this moment as another thing to be grateful for. She liked living in a city where she could enjoy both shopping and nature. The pond was unexpectedly located within 'Central Park.' 'Central Park,' as it was called, was a winding shopping center with acres of stores and restaurants. It had been a farm years before. Some people complained that it was now far too crowded with shoppers and stores and that they always got lost in it. But Anna enjoyed all that it had to offer. She tended to shop on weekdays when it was less crowded, and she'd learned the best ways to navigate through the twists and turns. Anna found it bright, clean and full of potential yummies.

"Look, Mommy, a duck butt!" Anna was pulled out of her musings by Lucy's delighted laughter. She'd spotted a duck feeding underwater with its little feathered tail end stuck up in the air. Anna and Adam used to joke about 'duck butt spottings' in college, with the ducks that frequented Crim Dell pond on the campus of William and Mary. That seemed a million years ago!

"I'm hungry, Mommy," Lucy suddenly announced. She'd had her fill of bird watching.

"Okay," Anna said, standing and stretching, "why don't we head for lunch?"

.... That night while the girls splashed in the large garden tub of the master bathroom, Anna stretched out on her bed in the adjoining room to read more of her grandmother's journal. She'd been startled to realize that with all of her work on gratitude, she hadn't picked up the journal in nearly a week. Turning to the next entry, she noticed that it was dated several months after the last one.

July 17, 1955

I'm not really sure what to write. I've been pretty miserable for months now, and I don't know what to do about it. The worst part is that I feel like I'm somehow preventing my own happiness, and I don't know what I'm doing. Lord, I need my life to change. I'm always tired, lonely, bored, overwhelmed and completely stuck in the everyday drudgery of being a housewife. What do I do to enjoy life?

..... Annie, the key to your change is your mind-- specifically, your thoughts. Pause for a minute and consider what you've been thinking about. It's all been about how miserable you are, right? I want you to be happy, even more than you want it for yourself! But, I can't do it without your help. You must begin by paying attention to your thoughts and your words. If you're only thinking and talking about being miserable, how can you expect to be anything else? How can I help you when I can't 'get in' past all that negativity? You have been granted free will in your actions and thoughts. I can't move in and 'brainwash' you. Whatever you're constantly focusing on is what you're going to see. Begin today by noticing what you're thinking, what you're saying. The

102

next step will be to replace those thoughts and words with ones of what you want to see in your life instead of what you don't want. We'll do this together! Just take that first step--notice what you're focusing on.

Anna paused in her reading to think over the implications of this idea. She knew she'd been as guilty as Annie of focusing on all that made her unhappy. 'I'm overweight and sick of it;' 'I don't have a rewarding career to return to now that the girls are older;' 'I'm a thirty-something frumpy housewife with nothing exceptional to offer...' If dwelling on these thoughts just reinforced them, then she truly had been her own worst enemy for years now! She felt like knocking herself in the forehead--one of those 'duh!' moments (or, 'I coulda had a V8!). Anna's thoughts were momentarily interrupted by her daughters' voices. She heard Martha explaining, "...so, this water in the tub is a liquid and see this bar of soap? That's a solid!" Martha had been learning about states of matter in school. It's all she could talk about lately. Anna then heard the sound of bubbles. Lucy exclaimed, "I just farted out gas!" Martha erupted in a burst of mixed giggles and "Uh-h-h!" Anna chuckled to herself and then returned to her previous line of thinking. She slowly

103

began to feel excited. If she had unwittingly kept herself unhappy for so long, what would happen if she were to change those habitual thoughts? Anna was glad that she was meeting with Charlotte and Barbara again tomorrow. She thought she had a new experiment to suggest for them.....

CHAPTER FIVE

At first all three women sat in the booth at the coffee shop glancing nervously at one another. Anna felt she was in school and the teacher had asked for a volunteer to share their book report aloud. In the next instant all three began talking at once and then laughed. The awkwardness had passed.

"So, what did you all think? What happened with the gratitude experiment?" Anna asked her friends, still somewhat anxious.

"I kept forgetting, the first few days," Charlotte admitted. Barbara and Anna nodded. "So, I put some little neon post-its around the house and in the car that said 'gratitude.' David thought I was crazy. One day I saw Charlie, my five year old, walking around with one stuck to his sweatshirt!" Charlotte laughed. "Anyway, the notes did the trick. By mid-week I didn't need them so much."

"Yeah, I wore a really jangly, annoying bracelet to help me remember. The problem was it was too annoying. I couldn't wait to yank the thing off! But, it worked, too," Anna confessed. Both women looked at Barbara. After a moment Barbara sighed, "Okay, okay, I admit it. I kept forgetting the first couple of days, too, but I didn't really do anything about it. Then, suddenly it was Tuesday and I knew I'd better start or Anna would strangle me," Barbara joked. "So, I sat a notebook on my bedside table and each night jotted down little things that happened that day I was grateful for."

"So, what happened once you started remembering to be grateful?" Anna asked, looking at both women. She took a lingering sip of her coffee, trying to appear nonchalant. The truth was she was bursting to share her revelations first, but she didn't want to influence their comments.

Charlotte began, "It didn't make a huge, huge difference, but it made a difference, you know what I mean?" Anna nodded encouragingly. Charlotte continued, "Like I said, at first David thought I'd lost it, but by the end of the week I was turning him on."

"What?!" Anna and Barbara chorused, causing a few heads to turn in their direction.

"Well, I was happier, less prickly, I guess, and I was paying more attention to him, to us. I was warmer and more approachable, so he approached," Charlotte said with a sly grin.

"I found the same sort of thing," Anna said. When Barbara looked at her with a raised eyebrow, Anna hurried on, "Not exactly that sort of thing. I mean that Adam and Lucy both commented on how much happier I seemed. It was helping my outlook, but also their relationship with me."

"No one said anything at my house," Barbara admitted, sounding a little defeated. She toyed absently with her half eaten muffin before confessing, "But, then, I guess I deliberately didn't draw a lot of attention to what I was trying." Barbara paused a moment while her friends waited patiently. "I don't want to hurt your feelings, Anna, but I felt kinda silly. I mean, what's the point, really? Isn't it just a bunch of mind games?"

Anna was initially somewhat hurt by her friend's skepticism, but she was also glad Barbara felt comfortable enough to be honest.

"Well, did you notice anything different about how you felt, how life was?" Anna questioned, hoping to salvage something out of the whole experience for her friend.

Barbara thought intently for a few moments before slowly stating, "I guess it did make the mundane parts of the day a little better."

"I found that, too!" Charlotte added, nearly spilling her hot tea in her eagerness. "I mean, even loading the dishwasher seemed a little yummier when I took a second to appreciate not having to wash it all by hand!"

"And I noticed, "Anna spoke up, not wanting to lose the forward thrust of the discussion, "that I even found myself feeling more generous. I admit I didn't always act on it, not yet, at least. But, there were times when I felt so blessed that the natural thing to do seemed to be to share it. I've found myself thinking I should do little things--baby-sit for the Harrison's so they can get out together without their new baby; bag up a bunch of the toys and books the girls have outgrown and see if a local church preschool or nursery could use them-- you know, simple things that wouldn't take a lot of time."

Turning to Barbara, Anna said carefully, "I do know what you're saying. But, I think there is a point to all of this. Being truly and consciously aware of all the ways you've been blessed makes life so much richer. Not only do you end up being happier right where you are, but I believe it opens the floodgates to more and more blessings." Was it Anna's imagination, or was Barbara avoiding her eyes? Anna felt a moment of panic. The last thing she wanted to do in all of this was to alienate one of her closest friends by preaching to her.

"Barbara," Charlotte intervened, "you know that this is all meant to be fun, right? It's not like having to pass an exam or anything. You don't have to do any of this. It's okay."

"I know," Barbara said, maybe a little curtly. What she wasn't saying was that she didn't want to be left out. She not only wanted to stay close to Anna and build a friendship with Charlotte, but she also felt deep down that her friends were onto something. She just had trouble shaking the thought that maybe it was all some kind of temporary brainwashing. Was there anything real and lasting about it? Or, were they just trying to kid themselves that there was anything magical about mundane life?

Anna was sitting, sipping her coffee with inner struggles battling on as well. She had planned to introduce a new 'experiment' today. How would Barbara

109

react? Should she just bag it? As the awkward silence stretched, Anna finally decided to press on. Anything had to be better than this!

"I've been reading more of my grandmother's journal," Anna began as an introduction to her 'thought experiment.' Charlotte looked at her expectantly. Barbara tried to look interested, but Anna thought she detected a hit of wariness in her gaze.

"She has some very interesting things to say about our thoughts. She says that our thoughts have power. Essentially whatever we're thinking about all the time and focusing on, we're creating in our lives. So, if we want something to change in our lives, we need to change our thoughts about it." Anna paused for her friends to have a chance to digest this new information, all the while acutely aware of their penetrating gaze. Anna continued, "I know it takes a bit to get used to, but it does make sense. For example, it's like me wanting to lose weight. I've been trying to for years, and I keep cycling up and down, winding up where I started. I'm beginning to think now the trouble hasn't been the wrong diet or even lack of motivation on my part. The problem has been how I've been thinking about it. All of my focus

110

has been on hating my body and the struggle involved in losing pounds. Now, I don't know--I haven't tried it yet, but what if I first worked on changing my thoughts?"

"So, you mean," Charlotte began excitedly, "change your thoughts to a more positive perspective. Focus, instead, on loving your body and how good you feel when you've worked out or when you feel a little lighter."

"Yes, exactly! And it could be on any topic, relationships, money, work, whatever. The key is to start paying attention to what you're thinking and what you're always talking about. Then, you begin systematically replacing those habitual thoughts that have held you back to more positive ones that move you to the change you want."

"So, is that our next experiment?" Barbara asked guardedly.

"Well," Anna hesitated, "I thought it would be worth a try. We could at least begin noticing our thoughts and make substitutions only if you want to."

"I think that sounds very interesting," Charlotte said pensively.

'You would,' Barbara thought cattily and then immediately felt ashamed. She knew that she was envious of Charlotte and her ability to theorize with Anna. Barbara had never been much on philosophy just for the sake of it. She was more of a practical do-er. But, Anna was trying to argue that this wasn't just philosophy--that it brought about real changes in the physical plane, the hear-and-now. Well, what could it hurt?

"You know, I think we're forming our own club," Charlotte continued.

"Are you kidding?" Barbara said incredulously.

Anna giggled, "Yeah, like Martha's nature club. Except, anyone who deliberately steps on a bug is thrown out." Barbara and Charlotte laughed. Then, to her friends' amazement, Barbara suggested, "We'll be the Philosophical Femmes!"

"Or, the Wondering Women," laughed Charlotte.

"The Thoughtful Friends!"

"The Gutsy Guessing Gals!"

"How about the Enlightened Ladies Club?" asked Barbara.

"I love it," agreed Anna.

"Great!" said Charlotte.

"Here's to the Enlightened Ladies!" said Anna, raising her mug. All three women clinked their coffee cups together.

"Wait a minute," said Barbara suddenly. Anna's heart sank. "Next week is Thanksgiving. I've got family coming to stay. Can we push our next meeting back a week?" Anna was immeasurably relieved. She'd thought Barbara was about to change her mind.

"Gosh, that's right. We're driving up to Massachusetts. Hours and hours with all four of us squeezed in the jeep, just to visit my neurotic relatives!" Charlotte said, laughing a little desperately.

"What a great opportunity to do the thought experiment!" Anna pointed out.

"Yeah, if it works through that trip, I'll be a life-long believer!"

"We're leaving town, too," Anna remembered aloud. "We always drive out to my aunt and uncle's house in the country. Why don't we try for the following Friday?"

"Sure."

"Okay."

113

.... Anna was standing in the bedroom looking around in dismay. She had piles of pants, shirts and sweaters stacked all over the bed, surrounding an empty suitcase. Trying to decide what to pack for Thanksgiving weekend was proving agonizing. Anna's entire extended family on her mother's side always gathered for Thanksgiving, so it was really more like a family reunion. Anna wanted to feel good about herself. She was always immensely proud of Adam and her girls, but since putting on weight, she just wanted to push them forward as her 'representatives' and then sit herself in the car for the duration. Her family was always accepting and loving; it was only Anna criticizing herself. She stood there hopelessly surveying her options. The tops weren't quite so bad. She had a handful of ones that were relatively flattering, 'as flattering as anything is on a chubby person,' she thought. The pants, however, were the rub, no pun intended. She had her stack of ones that were well worn standbys, size 16. Then, she had the 14's, some she could wear okay if she sucked in her stomach. She even had a stack of 12's, though most of them were out of the question unless she, say, ate nothing all weekend. This was Thanksgiving we were talking about, though. Anna

114

found herself drowning in a sea of miserable thoughts. 'I hate this;' 'If I were thin, I could look great in anything; instead, who am I kidding?' 'No matter what I wear, I'm not fooling anyone.' 'I'm sick of wearing the same things all the time because I don't even fit into most of what's in my closet.'

Suddenly the bedroom door swung open and Adam rushed in. Anna glanced at the clock: 6:30. She'd completely lost track of time. Adam had just gotten home from work.

"Hi dear--" Anna stopped speaking abruptly. Adam was hurriedly stripping.

"What are you doing?!" Anna thought for half a second that Adam was hoping for a quick rendezvous, with the girls right downstairs.

"I just treated a kid with the worst case of head lice I've ever seen!" Now down to his birthday suit, Adam grabbed his pile of clothes and held them at arm's length. Anna watched his bare butt shuffle down the hall as he dumped his clothes in the washer and then headed for a scalding shower. She erupted in giggles. Being a doctor wasn't always a prestigious as people imagined!

Laughing at Adam, Anna realized she was standing there scratching her own head.

Anyway, at least the interruption had ended her dismal thoughts about herself. She sat on the bed and pondered a moment how she should approach all of this, in light of the 'though experiment.' Well, the first part was pretty easy, noticing what her current thinking was about. Her day-to-day thoughts about her body and appearance were extremely negative! So, how could she, in this situation, think better thoughts? She certainly couldn't kid herself that she was comfortable yet in size 12, or even some 14's. Somehow, she had to find a better way of thinking about herself, even as a size 16. 'Yeah, right,' was her first thought. Well, Anna figured she probably needed to get away from sizes, period, at least for now. So, she quickly scooped up all the clothes on the bed that were way too small for her right now and pushed them out of sight. They certainly didn't make her feel any better yet. Left with only the clothes that were comfortable, Anna decided to choose outfits for the weekend like she would decorate a room, combining pleasing shades and textures. She tried to look at her familiar clothes with a new eye, letting go of the thoughts

116

over how big or small each item was. In a relatively short time Anna had pulled together three outfits she was pleased with. They were her standby clothes, but pairing tops, blazers and slacks differently, throwing in a scarf or necklace here and there, they looked new and almost chic. A grueling, self-deprecating task had been pleasant, and Anna actually found herself looking forward to sporting these outfits before her relatives.

Just as she placed the last article of clothing in the suitcase, Lucy pranced in the room.

"Whatcha doin', Mommy?"

"I'm packing for our trip. We're going to Aunt Paula's for Thanksgiving, and then we'll spend the weekend with Granny and Grandma."

"Yay!" Lucy and Martha loved spending time with their grandmothers. Gratefully, they lived within five miles of each other in Richmond, so it was convenient to visit both in the same weekend.

While Anna pulled together her toiletries in the bathroom to pack, Lucy wandered over to the scales. Stepping on, Lucy looked down at the numbers and asked, "How tall is I'm, Mommy?"

117

Anna grinned. "You're, uh, 35 pounds, Lucy."
Her younger daughter was such a lightweight! Anna
didn't even want to consider what her entire weight was.
Then she paused a moment. Here was another
opportunity to work on her thoughts. She knew that any
time she glanced at those scales, the number 160-
something flashed in her mind. She could almost
visualize 150-something, because she had actually been
that 'small' before. She really couldn't imagine standing
on the scales and seeing her ideal weight, more like 130.
Acting on impulse, Anna rushed out of the room.

"Where are you goin' Mommy?"

"I'll be right back--hold on!" A moment later she
reappeared with a strip of masking tape and a marker.
Carefully covering the digital screen with the tape, Anna
wrote 130 boldly on top. Lucy peered curiously over her
mother's shoulder.

"What are ya doin'?"

"Now, I don't want you to go taping or writing
over anything, okay? I'm just doing this to help me get to
the weight I want to be."

"Oh," said Lucy, sounding confused.

118

To help organize her own thoughts as much as anything, Anna explained, "To get to the size I want to be, I need to focus on where I want to end up, not where I've been. So, I'm going to keep this 130 number in my mind. I'll see it over and over on these scales 'till I can believe it's coming true."

"Like magic?" Lucy asked excitedly.

"Yeah, kind-of like magic."

"Mommy!" Martha called excitedly, rushing up the stairs and into the room. "I've got great news!" Martha had been playing at Ellen's house ever since stepping off the bus.

"What is it?" Anna put her suitcase on the floor and sat herself on the bed in its place.

"What you said worked! I kept thinking I'd do great on my math test, and I did! For the first time I finished all the problems before time was called, and I only missed one," Martha positively beamed.

"That's fantastic, sweetie!" Anna gave Martha a hug, with Lucy pushing her way in as well.

"I told Ellen about it, and she said maybe it would help her in school, too."

119

'Boy, what have I started?' thought Anna. Adam walked in wrapped in his robe and dripping on the floor. "What's all the yelling about?" he asked.

Before anyone could answer, Lucy peered closely at her mother and asked, "Mommy, why are you scratching your head?"

"No reason," Anna said, smiling sheepishly at Adam.

....　"I don't want curly hair," Lucy stated crossly.

"Yeah, but what does that have to do with your bread?" Anna asked. They were standing in Aunt Paula's kitchen by the trash can. It was Thanksgiving Day. Everyone else was seated in the dining room, enjoying their feast. Anna had missed Lucy, and after a brief search found her in the kitchen tearing the crust off her bread and pitching it in the trash.

"Miss Susan says this part of the bread makes your hair curly if you eat it," Lucy explained, systematically dissecting her bread.

"Oh, well, sweetie, she just said that to make you want to eat the crust."

"But I don't want curly hair."

120

"It doesn't make your hair curly."

"Yes it does! Katie ate hers, and her hair's curly!"

Anna could have pointed out that Katie's hair had always been curly, but she didn't want to prolong this ridiculous argument. Heading back to the table with Lucy and her naked bread slice, Anna mentally cursed Miss Susan's well-meaning advice. From now on Lucy would be destroying all of her sandwiches.

Seated once again in front of her turkey, Anna was glad she hadn't decided to wear her size 12 pants. On the other hand, she found she didn't have a great appetite, anyway. She was feeling depressed. She had begun the day feeling good about herself. She took extra time with her curling iron and make-up. She chose tan slacks, a chocolate brown blouse and a gold and olive silk scarf. She finished off the ensemble with simple gold hoop earrings and a splash of a musky perfume. Anna was pleased with the result and entered her aunt's house with pride. Fifteen minutes later, however, the arrival of her cousin, Tricia, sent her pride plummeting. The former plump and dumpy Tricia had been magically replaced by a trim, fit version. Apparently she had spent the past year

121

dieting and exercising, and the results were dramatic. Of course, everyone immediately oohed and aahed over the transformation, including Anna. If anyone had cared to look closely, though, they'd see Anna's smile was forced and frozen on her face. She knew she should be pleased for Tricia, but she felt angry and somehow ridiculously betrayed, as if all pudgy people shared an agreement to remain united against the skinny enemy. Losing weight and crossing over to their side was paramount to treason. Suddenly Anna's carefully chosen outfit seemed a pitiful, vain attempt for a dumpy person to look stylish. She felt Tricia, in her simple turtleneck and tiny jeans looked ten times more fashionable; it had nothing to do with style or color sense and everything to do with size. It was so unfair! Thin people looked good in anything, with no effort. Anna was perfectly aware her negative thoughts were raging out of control. In that moment, she could care less. She was filled with anger, an anger she silently aimed at Tricia, though she knew full well deep down that she was truly angry with herself.

Anna pushed her food around on the plate, not unaware of the irony; her anger over not losing weight was causing a loss of appetite.

122

"And so," Uncle Ted continued regaling the tale of his and Paula's latest trip to Washington, D.C., a true story of two country mice visiting the big city. "I couldn't find a parking spot and we were starving. I told Paula, 'Just let me drop you off at that McDonalds, and I'll drive back to pick you up.' What we didn't realize at the time was that we were in the red light district!"

Everyone laughed as Paula picked up the story, "So, Ted dropped me off and I got our food. I stood out front near the street, waiting for him to circle back. I started to get suspicious because lots of cars were driving by slowly. Then I looked closer at the women on each side of me. They had tube tops, miniskirts, stiletto heels, the whole works! Just about then Ted drove up and I jumped in the car and said, 'Let's get out of here!'". The family roared with laughter. Anna even chuckled at the image of her middle-aged, stoutly built aunt standing among prostitutes, clutching her McDonald's bag and waiting to be picked up. The laughter made Anna feel a little lighter. She adored her family. She thought of Charlotte, dreading the day with the group she termed her 'neurotic family members.' Many people felt that way, actually. Anna's extended family consisted of colorful

123

characters, all of whom had experienced their fair share of problems. Still, there seemed to be an unstated understanding that everyone left their problems at home on these special occasions. Some people may see it as false, but Anna was glad she never had to fear conflicts, bad feelings and embarrassing scenes at her family's gatherings. For the most part everyone truly did get along with one another.

As the desserts were being passed around, Anna found herself missing Faith. This year, Faith had accompanied her husband, Matt to his family's place in Pennsylvania. 'Of course,' pondered Anna bitterly, 'if Faith were here, everyone would be talking about her pregnancy and the little one on the way.' She realized with a little pang that once her thoughts jumped on the track to negativity, they seemed to snowball as they tumbled downhill. Even so, at that moment is seemed to Anna it would require a tremendous effort to stop that snowball in its tracks. She paused a moment to consider-- maybe it was worthwhile, after all, to try changing her thoughts to better ones. Just then she glanced over to see Tricia decline the offer of a dessert, choosing instead to sip her coffee. Anna looked down at her own mostly

124

eaten piece of pumpkin pie with whipped cream. 'Oh, forget it,' she thought angrily. She polished off every crumb of the pie in pure defiance and gladly embraced each negative thought that sprouted in her head.

.... Anna watched picturesque fields and farmhouses fly past in a blur, unable to appreciate any of the view. Adam had headed for his parents' house as soon as the Thanksgiving meal was finished, to visit them and spend the night at their house. Martha and Lucy had opted to spend the night with Anna's mom and to visit Adam's parents the next day. Having both sets of grandparents in the same town, they often flip-flopped about who spend the night where. Normally, Anna would have preferred the girls to have gone with Adam, so she could spend time alone with her mom. Tonight, though, she was glad of their distracting company. She had an exceptionally close relationship with her mother, but Anna wasn't in the mood for a heart-to-heart. She had endured rather than enjoyed the remainder of the day at Paula and Ted's house. Now, as her mother drove them all from Brookneal to Richmond, Anna longed to retreat to 'her' room and wallow in her misery.

125

"Let's play 'animal' twenty questions!" Martha suggested. They often played this travel game to pass the time, but always with the theme of animals for Martha's benefit.

"Kay! I got one!" Lucy immediately volunteered.

"Alright, Lucy," Granny said, over Martha's loud sigh.

"Is it a mammal?" Martha asked grudgingly.

"No, it's an animal with four legs, a tail, and it says 'bark.'" Lucy always volunteered so much information that the answer was obvious.

"It's a dog," Martha stated matter-of-factly.

"Yeah! Good job! How'd ya know?"

Martha rolled her eyes. "Okay, I've got one."

"Is it a mammal?" Granny asked.

"No."

"Is it a cat?" asked Lucy.

"No, Lucy, a cat's a mammal."

"Is it a bird?"

"No."

"Is it a horse?" wondered Lucy.

"No, Lucy! A horse is a mammal, too!"

"Is it a kind of fish?"

"No."

"Is it a rabbit?" Lucy ventured.

"No, Lucy!"

"Is it a reptile?"

"Yes."

"An alligator?"

"No."

"A snake? A lizard? A gecko?"

"No, no, no."

"Martha," Granny finally said, "would we even know what this animal is?"

"It's a blue-tongued skink!" Martha revealed triumphantly. While Lucy made her animal choice too simple, Martha inevitably made hers too obscure.

Eventually the hour and a half drive was over, and they arrived at Granny's house. Anna found her mother's house to be infinitely comforting. It was a tiny ranch style home with white siding and blue shutters. Anna and Faith had grown up in this house from age eight. This had been the first and only house their mother owned by herself since the divorce. Everything in the tiny three bedroom, one bath home was worn and shabby.

127

The mauve carpet had turned the color of melted Neapolitan ice cream: chocolate, strawberry and vanilla blended together. The walls still had the silhouettes of pictures moved and never replaced; the couch had a sheet as a slipcover and plywood boards to support the cushions; the garbage disposal didn't work; the faucet dripped into the stained tub and the front yard was more dirt than grass. Nevertheless, when Anna dreamed of an escape, her mother's house came to mind over a seaside resort or an upscale hotel. Because, on that carpet Anna and Faith had crawled around pretending to be cats, or sometimes building pillow forts in the middle of the floor. The couch had served as everything from a boat for Martha's seafaring expeditions to a springboard for Lucy's gymnastics. Martha and Lucy splashed and played in the tub together just as Anna and Faith had years before. And, Anna's girls preferred dirt to grass in the front yard. For Martha, in particular, it was ideal. On dry days her toy animals could be in the desert. After a rainy spell there were excellent puddles and mud for the animals to muck about in.

The comfort of her mother's house was about more than playful memories, though. There was a feeling

128

of peace and acceptance. No room was off limits; there were no formalities to observe; it was a make-yourself-at-home and come-as-you-are kind of place, and Anna was always a bit sad and anxious to leave it to return to 'the real world.'

This night, in particular, Anna wrapped herself in the comfort of her room, willing the bad feelings to go numb. She could hear her mother and the girls playing in the living room. It made her feel a little better knowing her daughters were enjoying themselves. Anna propped up the pillows on the bed and slid under the ivory sheets and duvet. She had the TV tuned to an old black and white movie quietly in the background. She loved movies made in the '30's and '40's, especially mysteries and comedies. She found comfort in watching people move about through what she believed must have been simpler times, even if they weren't, really. She pulled her newest library book into her lap, but found she couldn't concentrate on the book or the movie.

What had been her problem today? She had begun the day in such high spirits. Tricia showing up thinner couldn't have been the only cause of Anna's current misery. She thought back over her day in search

129

of where things went so wrong. Obviously, Tricia's new look served as a very concrete reminder to Anna of the change she wanted for herself. Instead of being excited and expectant about those same results for herself someday, though, Anna had chosen to focus on the fact that she wasn't there yet. That awareness of her lack of a fit body had grown to anger, disappointment, self-chastisement and the defeated belief that she would never have that body. Then, like weeds springing up and choking out blooms, her thoughts had spread to all the changes in her life that hadn't yet happened. By the end of the day she was left feeling destitute, as if it had become a certainty that none of her hopes and dreams would ever come to fruition. 'This is ridiculous,' Anna thought, 'I'm feeling and acting like there's been some great tragedy in my life! My life is the same as it was this morning. I've condemned myself in my head, that's all. I could just as easily lift that doomed sentence and change it to a proclamation of good.'

Anna took a deep breath. She felt she'd just been given a pardon by the governor at the eleventh hour. She still wasn't feeling good about her size 16 body, and she still desired great positive changes in her life to shout to

130

the world. But, at least those desires were a little less of an ache and more of a hope. She supposed part of her anger had been due to frustration and impatience. She had felt so much better during their gratitude experiment. She somehow wanted that improved outlook to lead immediately to an improved life. Tricia's trim figure brought all of Anna's impatience bubbling to the surface.

"Momma, Momma, come here!" Martha's voice cut through Anna's thoughts.

"I'm coming," Anna called, pulling back the covers.

"What is it?" Anna entered the living room to find her mother and the girls seated before an open cedar chest. Apparently they'd decided to do a little exploring into the past. All sorts of paraphernalia spilled out, everything from old yearbooks to school diplomas to Anna and Faith's original Holly Hobby and Cabbage Patch dolls.

"Look at all this, Momma!" Martha was pouring through old black and white family photos. Lucy was busy admiring the old dolls, hoping to claim one as her own.

131

"Wow, Mom, I can't believe you held onto all this stuff!" Anna said, "Those dolls would be worth a pretty penny today, I bet."

"Can we keep them, Mommy?" Lucy begged, clutching a Cabbage Patch doll to her chest. "I don't want a pretty penny."

Anna smiled. "Yes, sweetie, I'd never get rid of those dolls." Turning to her mother, she said, "Remember how you had to almost literally fight to get those for us for Christmas?"

"Yes, I sure do!" Anna and her mother laughed together. Anna's laughter shopped short, though, as her eyes fell upon some familiar spindly handwriting.

"What is it?" asked Anna's mother.

Picking up a tattered folder, Anna glanced inside at sheets of paper covered in what she recognized as her grandmother's handwriting. "What is this?" Anna asked her mother.

"I think it's some essays or something my mother wrote. She was often writing, every spare chance she got. I'd forgotten I had those."

"Would you mind terribly if I looked at them? I could made copies and leave the originals with you."

132

"Sure, whatever, sweetie." Anna's mother looked a bit confused.

"See, Mom, I recently found Granny's journal, and I've been reading it. Have you read any of her writings?"

"No, not really. I know I should have, but I guess with her being my mother, I felt kind-of funny. It seemed too personal, somehow, even with her gone."

"Do you mind me reading them?"

"Heavens, no!"

"It's just, she's got a lot of interesting things to say, some very helpful ideas."

"Really?"

"Yeah. I'll keep on reading, and at some point we'll have to have some time to ourselves, and I'll tell you about them."

"Okay."

"Come on, Granny, let's play!" chorused Martha and Lucy.

"I'm gonna go back and read some. Is that okay, Mom? Just yell if you need me," Anna said.

"Sure, dear, go ahead."

Anna hurried back to her spot on the bed and settled in to read the first sheet of paper she came to. Each page had a title on top. These did appear to be more like short essays than diary entries. Gazing at the now so familiar handwriting, the Twilight Zone theme song popped into Anna's head. It seemed quite coincidental that Annie McDowell's writings should appear again, particularly after the day she had put herself through. Was her grandmother trying to speak to her from the grave, as some sort of guardian angel? That idea was a little more creepy than comforting. 'Anyway,' Anna thought, 'whatever's going on, I'll make the most of it!'

The top sheet Anna pulled out of the folder was entitled *'Writings from God'*:

One technique I sometimes use when I feel I need guidance is creating a 'conversation' with God. A friend clued me in to this exercise, and I have to admit that at first I was a bit skeptical. Essentially, I write to God, and God 'writes' back to me. I start by writing to God about whatever problems I may be having. I completely vent, whine, complain and express any and all anger and fear. I also ask for help. Then, I put down my pen and take a deep breath. I try to let go of the fear or anger, anxiety

134

and tension. I say a brief prayer for God to speak to me
and give me advice. Then, I pick up my pen and begin a
new sheet of paper. This time, I begin 'Dear Annie' and
write to myself whatever I feel God is trying to say. It
feels a little strange at first, but I try to free-write, not
thinking too hard or analyzing anything that 'comes out.'
What I generally find is that deep down inside me there is
a 'God presence.' It reassures me that all truly is well;
that God always provides; that I can be peaceful and let
go--all those truths that I know deep down, once I calm
down and step back a moment. Sometimes, I've even been
a little surprised by what 'I' write. It hasn't been anything
dramatic. I just mean that sometimes it will take a
different slant or focus than what was on my mind.

Once I feel that I've 'emptied' all I had to give, I
often put the writings aside for a little while. Later, even
after only an hour or later in the day, I re-read what 'God'
wrote. It's then that I realize my 'God presence' was
involved, for oftentimes I don't remember word-for-word
what was written. It's as if I'm truly reading it for the first
time.

'So, that explains her journaling technique,'
thought Anna. 'Maybe I should share it with Charlotte

135

and Barbara after all. I mean, whether you believe it's actually God 'writing' the words or simply allowing one's subconscious to 'speak' out, it does seem a clever way of getting into the truth of the matter.' She still wondered what Barbara's reaction would be, though. 'Oh well, she hasn't given up on me yet. I may as well plough ahead!'

Anna then pulled out the next piece of paper, entitled *'Consistency.'*

It's consistency that makes change. You have to consistently exercise to get in shape, and keep it up to stay there. You have to consistently eat healthy and light to lose weight and keep it up to stay trim. Couldn't the same be true of one's thoughts, attitudes and expectations? Of course it is! You can't expect to lose weight and keep it off if you only eat correctly here and there, and in the meantime you stick to old eating habits. Likewise, how can I expect great changes in my life if I'm only using the right thoughts and expectations intermittently, and all other times I'm thinking old thoughts? Another point: getting truly in shape or losing a fair amount of weight takes time. You have to be patient to see the full results. It's hard sometimes. You want to give up along the way. But, then you'll never reach your goals or enjoy the

136

results of all your work. I must also be patient to see the
final rewards of staying consistent with my thoughts. It
takes time to fully reap the rewards. But, if I quit along
the way, I'll never get there. Another point: in dieting
and exercising, it does take time to completely reach your
goals. But, all along the way are rewards of feeling
better, gaining energy, clothes fitting better and dropping
clothing sizes. Likewise, it will take some time to reach
all of my ultimate miracles. However, all along the way I
should begin feeling more peaceful and contented. I
should worry less and generally enjoy life more.

So, I need to be consistent. Now, that doesn't
mean I always have to have positive, lofty thoughts and
attitudes. But, I do need to believe in the best, in general.
And, during rough times or low times, my thoughts can
simply be 'I want life to feel better.'

When Anna put the sheet down, the Twilight
Zone music popped into her head again. That writing was
right on the money, as far as Anna's day had gone. Once
again, her grandmother was right. Whether losing weight,
getting in shape or changing your life, it doesn't happen
like winning the lottery-- instant millionaire overnight. It
takes time and it takes perseverance, remaining true and

137

consistent in reaching your ultimate goal. But the determination is worth it, because just as Annie pointed out, there are rewards all along the way. So, Anna needed to consistently envision 130 lbs. on her scales; consistently go to the YMCA; consistently work on holding positive thoughts regarding her body and consistently expect great changes in all areas of her life. The good will come!

Feeling worlds better than she did only an hour ago, Anna set aside the folder and glanced at the TV. 'Yes,' she thought, "The Thin Man' is coming on next!' Knowing her wonderful mother would go through the girls' nighttime routine for her, Anna settled back on the pillows for a rare chance to enjoy a movie uninterrupted.

CHAPTER SIX

"You told Charles to pee in his car seat?"
Barbara asked incredulously.

"Well, I really didn't have any other choice,"
Charlotte explained. The members of the Enlightened
Ladies Club had once again gathered for the latest
'meeting.' Charlotte added Splenda to her hot tea as she
continued, "We had worked our way from Boston all the
way down through New York City. We'd made a pit stop
not long before, but they were doing construction on the
bridge we needed, and we had to circle all through the
city to get on a different one. David and I were arguing,
and without noticing, Charles downed most of a bottle of
flavored water. So, finally, we were on the bridge to head
into New Jersey, and Charles announced he had to pee.
There was nowhere, not even the shoulder to pull over,
'cause there were cones set up. Charles was getting
desperate and crying, and traffic was at a standstill. So, I
told him to try and pee in the empty bottle. Unless I
literally climbed into the back, I couldn't reach him to
help. Well, anyway, he did the best he could, but his aim
wasn't great, and, well, it was a mess."

139

"I can imagine," stated Anna, actually trying not to imagine.

"Just as all this was happening, traffic moved and we were finally entering New Jersey. Well, you know how those factories stink? For one awful moment I wondered if Charles had done more than just pee. Then I realized where the smell was coming from," Charlotte summed up her story of the Thanksgiving trip from hell.

"Goodness! Was your whole vacation miserable?" Barbara asked.

"Pretty much, yeah. Well, that is, it was the same as it always is, but I did try to work on my thoughts. And, you know, it did help a bit. I mean, my family was as nutty as ever, and the drive was still long, but my attitude was 'I want to be amused, not annoyed.' It wasn't always easy, but I did laugh more at things, where before I would have cried or screamed."

Barbara still looked horrified at the thought of enduring Charlotte's Thanksgiving experience. Her hand had subconsciously gone to her throat, toying with the gold chain lying there. Anna didn't blame her; over the years Anna had heard Charlotte recount numerous road trips that would have sent Anna directly to a straight

140

jacket and a padded cell. Somehow, Charlotte endured it and managed to survive one 'vacation' after another.

"Well, I didn't have nearly as, um, 'exciting' a Thanksgiving as you did," Barbara began tactfully, "but for me it was just as much of a disaster."

"Oh no, not you, too! What happened?" asked Anna. She had already briefly shared her own miserable Thanksgiving Day, feeling angry about her size sixteen body. 'Bad news comes in threes,' she though, anxiously dissecting her cheese danish rather than eating it.

"I burned the turkey! I mean, I actually burned the flaming turkey!" Anna and Charlotte stared at their friend with their mouths gaping open. Barbara prided herself on her cooking. She was known for delicious, made-from-scratch comfort food. All of her family flocked to her home every Thanksgiving and Christmas to enjoy Barbara's excellent entertaining, warm hospitality and delicious baking. Anna knew it wasn't effortless on Barbara's part; her friend stressed a great deal about making it perfect, but her hard work always resulted in a Norman Rockwell kind of holiday.

"What happened?" Anna repeated.

141

Barbara took a large swig of coffee, as if it were a whiskey. "Chris had some cousins visiting, and he wanted to impress them, I suppose. So, he apparently chugged almost an entire liter of Mountain Dew all at once, with them cheering him on. Well, then, of course, he felt sick. He kept saying he needed to throw up but couldn't. I figured he essentially had a huge gas bubble and just needed some antacid or something. That didn't seem like a very macho solution to him. He kept trying to vomit instead. I finally got him to crunch a couple of Tums, and then, to the delight of the cousins, Chris let out a colossal, earth-shattering belch. Then he felt better. Anyway, this whole ridiculous saga went on for almost an hour, and I forgot to take out the turkey."

"What did you do?" Charlotte asked.

"It wasn't exactly completely burnt, but near enough. I managed to cut off the outer part that was black. What was left was awfully dry. That's not all, though. When I went to take the sweet potato casserole out of the oven and set it on the counter, I tripped over Freddie."

"Oh no," Anna knew how devoted Barbara was to Frederick III, her black daschund hound.

142

"Oh, yes. The casserole shattered and sweet potato with tiny marshmallows went flying." Charlotte choked on her tea, trying not to snort in laughter. Anna was also trying desperately not to smirk until she could tell what Barbara's reaction would be.

"You know, cleaning up that sweet potato, all I could think was 'how did all this fit into that casserole dish?' I swear there was enough sweet potato on my kitchen floor and walls to fill a barrel."

Seeing the hint of a grin playing on Barbara's lips, Anna finally allowed herself to chuckle. Pretty soon all three women were laughing right out loud.

"Well," Anna ventured as the laughter died down, "I'm scared to ask this, considering your stories, but what did you think of the thought experiment?" Anna glanced anxiously at Barbara, in particular.

Charlotte spoke right up, "I feel like I need a lot more work on it. But, I really do think there's something in it." She began to chew thoughtfully on her poppy seed bagel.

"Yes, I know what you mean," Anna agreed. "The one thing I definitely realized is our thoughts have a tremendous effect on our moods! And, it seems once

143

you're on the path of thinking good or bad, it gains momentum quickly."

"What do you mean?" Barbara asked, looking a little lost.

"See, when I started thinking how I was overweight and ugly and hated myself, the bad thoughts just grew and grew. By the end of the day I was angry, sad, miserable, and felt like everything in my life was a failure." Barbara looked sympathetically at her friend. "Then, when I began consciously changing my thoughts to how everything I want, including a thin body, is still possible, my mood lifted considerably! Pretty soon more good thoughts came pouring in." Anna paused a moment for emphasis. "Don't you see? Nothing had actually, physically happened throughout the day that was good or bad. It was all in my head; I had the option of making it good or bad, based on my thoughts and attitude."

"Yes," Charlotte leaned forward in her chair, getting into the discussion, "and with my awful trip, even though things outside myself were actually bad, I still had the choice of how it affected me. Instead of letting it make me angry or stressed, I tried to see the humor of it all." She smiled apologetically. "I didn't always succeed, but I tried."

"I feel like you must have done the same thing." Charlotte said to Barbara.

Barbara put her cup down without taking a drink and looked at Charlotte in surprise. "Why do you say that?"

"Well, you don't seem as upset as I thought you would over your food mishaps."

Anna smiled. She was sure Charlotte had no idea how much that remark probably meant to Barbara. Sure enough, she detected a glow of pride as Barbara confessed, "I did at least try to be aware of what my thoughts were. I didn't actually work on changing them, exactly. But, you know, just realizing your thoughts are negative almost puts a stop to them." Anna sheepishly remembered how she had defiantly embraced her negative thoughts for most of the day, but she knew what Barbara meant.

Feeling a flash of inspiration, Anna said, "You know what I think the key thing is in all of this?" Charlotte and Barbara stopped mid-chew to hear the announcement. "I think the main purpose is to live pro-

145

actively rather than re-actively." Her friends simply stared at her, so Anna pushed on. "I mean, most of the time we go through our days just reacting to what goes on around us. Our thoughts and moods form in reaction to our circumstances. I think what we're trying to do is change that. We want to put forth our own thoughts and moods deliberately first, and then see how our circumstances change for the better."

Barbara swallowed the last of her muffin before asking, "But do you really think our circumstances would change?"

"Well, I don't actually know." Anna sat back in her chair, feeling a little deflated.

"It's certainly worth a try," Charlotte piped up. "At the very least, you would feel better, no matter what the circumstances."

"Yes, but what's the point of feeling great while your world is still falling apart?" Barbara pointed out.

Needing to defend her epiphany, Anna argued, "I can't really explain or prove it, but I do think that if your thoughts, mood and outlook are greatly improved on a regular basis, then your circumstances would begin to improve, too. One of my grandmother's writings

146

emphasizes how important it is to be consistent. I don't think you can work on your thoughts a day here and there and expect to see your life change. I think it's crucial to stay consistent."

"This is starting to sound like an awful lot of work," Barbara said testily.

"Maybe at first, but it's like creating any habit; once the changes start to get familiar, it's not really any more work. I mean, you'll have the same number of thoughts a day, just different ones. And, think of the potential pay off! Wouldn't it be worth being pro-active about your thoughts if it meant actually creating your dream life?"

"But, do you really believe that's possible?"

Anna paused a moment before declaring, "Yes, I do."

"I hate to end our discussion, guys, but I'm gonna have to head out soon. What's our agenda for this week?" Charlotte asked, beginning to gather her coat and purse.

"Why don't we just keep working on our thoughts for now?" Anna suggested.

"Sounds good! I'm off now! I'll see you Enlightened Ladies next week."

"Bye, Charlotte," said Anna and Barbara. They then sat rather awkwardly together, each toying with the debris left on the table. Anna looked directly at her friend and said, "I don't want any of this to change things for us. I'm just excited at the idea of having more control over my life. It's the type of thing where talking it through with other people helps, 'cause it's such a different way of thinking. That's why I brought it up with you and Charlotte." Barbara said nothing, so Anna continued, "But, if it's ruining our friendship in any way, I'll keep it to myself. It's not worth that."

Barbara smiled. "Our friendship means a lot to me, too. That's why I've been trying to participate. This is obviously really important to you, Anna. How could I remain a close friend and not at least try to understand?" She paused thoughtfully a moment. "It's more than that, though. I am intrigued. I mean, who wouldn't want to have more of a say in creating their own life?"

Feeling somewhat encouraged, Anna said, "And, this isn't like black magic or anything. We're not performing rituals or praying to statues. The idea is that there is indeed a God, Spirit or Universal Power out there. And, I think when God said we're made in His image, He

148

meant that to more of a degree than we realize. I'm not saying we're mini-gods, but God says He's in us, right? I think that partly means that we have more power than we know, and God meant for us to have that power. I mean, experts say we use a very small percentage of our brains. What if God meant far more and better for us than we realize? What if, instead of begging for God alone to change things in our lives, He meant for us to join Him in the power He's given us and make the changes we want?"

Barbara took a deep breath. "That's quite a thought."

Anna grinned. "I know, I'm sorry; I'll stop lecturing. I'm just trying to make the point that I don't see all of this as something trendy or 'New Age.' I think it actually complements traditional religion...Anyway, I mainly want you and me to be okay. Are we?"

Barbara reached over and squeezed Anna's arm. "Yeah, we are."

.... Anna's stomach grumbled as she pulled out lettuce, tomato and an onion to dress up the burgers. Adam was grilling outside. Felling it was time to take some real action concerning her weight, Anna had begun

149

the Slimfast program--a bar or shake for breakfast and lunch, followed by a sensible dinner. She wasn't sure hamburgers were a sensible dinner, but she planned to allow herself only one burger. Also, in lieu of chips and mac and cheese sides, she'd sautéed green beans and mushrooms and prepared a fruit salad. She wasn't sure how the family felt about it, but she figured as long as she was making healthier choices, they may as well all benefit! So far the dieting hadn't been nearly as rough as she'd feared, especially considering it was the Christmas season. She allowed herself several snacks so-as not to feel deprived--one mid-morning, mid-afternoon and before bed. She tried to ensure that snacks were healthy and in small portions: nuts, fruit, yogurt, pretzels, cheese, popcorn, fresh veggies, etc. She also allowed herself one or two small sweets a day; it was the Christmas season after all! Despite the numerous allowances, Anna did feel her body becoming lighter. She had weighed herself at the beginning (even after bracing herself for the worst, she still gasped silently at the number glaring up at her.) She decided not to weigh herself again until she could tell real differences in the way her clothes were fitting. She wanted each weigh-in to show a big drop, until she reached her 130 goal.

"Mommy, Daddy needs a plate for the boogers," Lucy said, appearing at the top of the basement steps. Anna cringed slightly inside. Lucy never could manage to say 'burgers' clearly.

"Here you go," Anna handed a plate to Lucy, who ducked back down the stairs. Because the land sloped drastically, their front door was ground level, but their kitchen at the back of the house was one story up. The builders intended for owners to build a deck off of the kitchen, but Anna and Adam couldn't afford it. So, their grill had to sit outside at the back, an entire level down. Grilling became a relay event of traveling up and down the basement steps from the kitchen through the basement den, out to the back patio. Needless to say, they didn't grill very much.

Still, this was a quiet December Sunday afternoon. The football game was on; the Christmas tree had been put up the day before and stood proudly twinkling in the front picture window; nothing pressing was on the agenda, so they decided to indulge in the freshly grilled taste of summer in the winter. Anna had everything ready in the kitchen. All they needed were the

151

cooked burgers. Anna glanced out of the kitchen window down to the back patio. Adam stood there in his winter coat and gloves, flipping burgers in the December chill. Lucy was also outside, completely bundled. Anna could tell that Lucy was arguing with her dad about wanting to leave the patio door cracked, despite the draft. Lately she'd developed an absolute phobia about closed doors. She was convinced that every closed door was also locked. Anna felt bad; one would think they'd been locking Lucy in the closet or something. Nevertheless, she was driving them all crazy with it; she followed behind everyone in the house insisting that all doors remained cracked, even bathroom ones. Sometimes after the girls had gone to bed Anna and Adam closed and locked their bedroom door for obvious reasons. Anna worried that one of these times Lucy would awaken, find them 'locked in' and phone 911.

Anna's stomach grumbled again as she watched Adam check the burgers for doneness. She realized that before, her stomach never growled. She never allowed herself to get empty. Psychologists would probably argue she was trying to fill some void in her life. Whatever the reason, she was having to re-learn that it was okay to feel hungry rather than always feeling full. Adam removed all the patties onto the plate, and he and Lucy headed upstairs.

"Martha, dinner's ready!" Anna called up to the bedrooms. At the same moment everyone converged in the kitchen, absolutely ravenous.

"I want a big hambooger, Mommy!"

Martha giggled.

"Alright, Lucy."

.... Anna had cleaned up the kitchen and put the girls in the tub. While Adam cleaned up the patio and grill, she settled herself on the couch to peruse more of her grandmother's writings. She'd been so busy lately with the holidays that she'd neglected her 'learning' time. Even though it was still early in December, Anna made the most of absolutely every minute of the Christmas month. Growing up, Anna and Faith's mother didn't really have the extra time, energy and money it took to indulge in holiday festivities. Anna probably overcompensated a bit with her own children, but she loved it. As soon as November was behind them, all the autumn touches were replaced with winter ones. She played instrumental

153

Christmas CD's, lit pine-scented candles and exchanged her pumpkin-oriented recipes for ginger ones. December always involved sending fifty-odd Christmas cards, making gingerbread 'mans' as Lucy said, Christmas crafts and foods such as warm gingerbread, hot tea, hot chocolate and winter stews. Ironically, the girls didn't really eat stew or gingerbread very well, and Anna had yet to make a ginger cookie that wasn't truly hard enough to use as a building material. Still, hope springs eternal. Every year she made all the same foods and was slightly put out by the amount of stew, bread and cookies left uneaten.

Before Anna could choose an essay to read, the phone rang. Caller id let her know it was her in-laws.

"Hello?"

"Hi, Anna, it's Mike."

"Hi! How are ya?"

"I'm fine...is Adam around?"

"Sure, let me find him, " Anna said, grinning. Her father-in-law was a dear man, but he wasn't much for small talk, and he especially hated to chat on the phone. Anna headed downstairs and opened the back sliding glass door.

154

"It's your dad."

"Thanks. Hey, Pop. Yeah, what a game!"

Anna closed the door and headed upstairs just in time to hear angry yelling from above. Continuing up to the third floor, she entered the bathroom, panting a little. Who needed to go to the gym, with all these blasted steps?

"What's wrong, girls?"

"Mommy, she won't give back my imaginary puppy!" Lucy cried.

"What?"

"I let her look at my imaginary puppy, and now she won't give it back."

Anna looked at Martha, who had an expression on her face that was a blend of defiance, devilishness and amusement. For the most part Martha was a supportive, kind and loving big sister. At times, however, she was a very typical tormenting older sibling.

Feeling a bit foolish, Anna ordered, "Martha, give Lucy back her imaginary dog."

"It's a puppy, Mommy!"

"Right, give back the puppy."

155

Just then Anna's cell phone began beeping downstairs. With a sigh, she rushed down the steps once again and pulled her cell phone out of her purse. The caller id had her own home phone listed. Anna simply stood there staring stupidly at her cell phone, trying to figure out what was going on. Her phone stopped ringing, and a second later Adam's cell phone began ringing. Anna picked up his phone and saw a picture of herself. Adam had programmed in pictures of each person to match their phone number. Feeling at a complete loss, Anna stood there with a cell phone in each hand, trying to register how her home phone was calling her. Just then she heard banging downstairs. 'Oh no!' Anna suddenly realized, 'Adam's locked out!' Rushing down the stairs, she finally understood--when she'd handed Adam the phone earlier, she'd automatically locked the glass door. Anna rushed through the den, undid the latch and pulled open the door. Anna stood holding a cell phone in each hand, facing Adam, who was holding the cordless phone.

"Thanks a lot," he said.

After a hasty explanation, Anna rushed back upstairs, where she heard more arguing. Entering the bathroom laughing and panting, she told the girls about

156

the phone mix up. Without thinking, she blurted out the part about having locked Adam outside. Lucy's eyes grew as large as saucers. Anna had to spend twenty minutes reassuring her that she'd unlocked the door and Daddy was fine.

.... 'Finally, finally, finally,' thought Anna. The girls had finished their bath and been tucked into bed. Anna had changed into pj's and shut herself in the bedroom with quiet music playing and the folder of her grandmother's papers. Choosing a sheet at random, Anna read *'Attraction'* at the top. For a moment she wondered if her grandmother had branched into dating advice until she began reading.

As I've grown older, I've been able to enjoy the benefits of hindsight. One major thing I've noticed is how people tend to attract the same things into their lives over and over again, even if it's something that makes them unhappy. People with health problems seem to keep having health issues; people who have run-ins with the law keep returning to crime; people born into poverty tend to stay there. The same is true on the opposite end. Wealthy people seem to get richer; successful people continue to climb the ladder; healthy people tend to remain strong and robust into old age.

As for myself, I struggled most of my life with fears over money. My husband I cycled up and down in our finances for decades, never seeming to get ahead for long. Then, there's a friend of mine who used to worry all the time about the safety of her children, to an obsessive degree. Sure enough, her kids did have more injuries and near misses than any children I've heard of. Knowing the power that our thoughts and beliefs have in our lives, I've begun to realize the things that keep happening to us are not random. It's not good luck or bad luck. Not only do our repeated thoughts create things in our lives, but they draw more of those types of things to us. So, repeated thoughts of prosperity not only create prosperity, but draw more opportunities for prosperity. Likewise, focusing upon health problems creates them and draws more poor health issues to you. Like magnets, we attract people, events and circumstances into our lives that match what we expect to see. The wonderful thing about that is we can change what we're attracting. Begin focusing your thoughts and words on what you want to see in your life and it will be drawn to you!

158

Anna put the essay down with the Twilight Zone music running through her head again. This idea of 'attraction' sure would explain a lot! Anna remembered how she'd been seeking some sort of answers in her life and then 'stumbled' across the journal. Then, at another low point on Thanksgiving, she'd uncovered the essays, seemingly at random. What else could she be drawing into her life this very moment? Anna initially cringed at that thought. It brought to mind the Ghostbusters movie and Dan Ackroyd's character whose thoughts inadvertently create a smiling, skyscraper sized marshmallow monster to destroy the city. But, no, Anna didn't want to be afraid of her thoughts. Everyone had a million random ideas pass through their heads--good, bad and in between. It didn't mean they wanted any of it to enter into their lives for real. No, Anna decided, random thoughts that occur can just pass on through. She figured it was only when you give a thought power by dwelling on it that you drew it into your life.

As Anna got up to go brush her teeth, she began to think--maybe she should devote some time deliberately attracting what she wanted. Perhaps she should pray or meditate. She'd heard that athletes often visualize

159

themselves successfully executing their event or sport. Maybe she should visualize herself as thin, wealthy, successful and contented in a new home. That could be fun, like day-dreaming with a purpose!

Anna climbed back in bed, but wasn't quite ready to sleep yet. She decided to read one more essay before calling it a day. The paper she pulled out of the folder was entitled *'Feelings'*.

Through much of our lives we're taught to disregard our feelings. They're seen as fickle things, completely unreliable and useless when compared to reason, logic and intellect. Women, in particular, are chastised for letting their emotions rule their heads. But, surely, there's a purpose to our feelings. God gave them to us, after all. I can't imagine their only purpose is to prevent humans from behaving robotically. No, I've come to believe that feelings work with attraction, just as our thoughts do. When you feel happy, you attract more situations to feel happy about. The same is true of depression or anger, as well. Not only that, but our feelings act as a gauge to tell us where we are in our thoughts. If you feel bad, then your thoughts must be dwelling on the negative. So, it's important to feel happy;

160

to feel loving; to feel gratitude and appreciation. When we have those feelings, we know we're drawing more goodness into our lives. In that sense our feelings hold more concrete value and information than logic or reason!

'Well,' thought Anna, 'that makes it easier; instead of analyzing every thought I have, I can simply focus on feeling good.' She turned off the light, put the folder on the floor and sunk down under the sheets. Adam always came to bed after her. Anna thought she'd take the opportunity to do some visualizing. Closing her eyes, she summoned a clear picture of a slim, fit version of herself wearing slacks and a blouse actually tucked in. Then she transferred 'herself' to the living room of her new dream home. There was a wood fire crackling in the fireplace, and their new cream sectional was facing it, flanked by two matching leather chairs in mahogany tones of brown. Glancing out the large windows, Anna only saw trees, lawn and privacy as far as the eye could see. During the visualization, Anna tried to create as many clear details as possible. She also tried to really feel as if it were a reality, along with all the accompanying excitement, pride and pleasure. She let 'herself' wander

161

into the kitchen, done in a mix of modern country and English style. It was full of creams, wood tones and terra cotta hues. It housed all of the extras she'd dreamed of: bead board; a central island with a sink; storage and barstools; a breakfast nook; large windows; a built-in plate rack and a small built-in desk. Lying there in bed, Anna found herself getting so excited, she knew she'd never sleep. She decided maybe this kind of visualization would be best in the mornings when she wanted to get pumped up for the day. Still, it had been fun!

Switching gears, Anna took a deep breath and decided to meditate a moment before drifting off to sleep. She focused solely on her breathing for a bit, feeling her body relax. Then, with each inhalation she thought the word 'peace' and with each exhalation she thought 'happiness.' She fell asleep feeling quite content.

.... "This is fun! I feel like we should be doing each other's hair and freezing someone's bra," Charlotte giggled.

"I'm not sure that our three bras would fit in the freezer," Barbara laughed, glancing at everyone's buxom chests. Anna carried over a tray of hot cocoa and

162

shortbread cookies to join her friends at her kitchen table. With Christmas only a week and a half away, the 'Enlightened Ladies Club' was finding it difficult to arrange a time to meet. So, Anna had managed to send Adam and the girls out for a Sunday afternoon. She had an activity planned for the club and didn't think a restaurant would work.

Charlotte looked at everything on the table: magazines, scissors, card stock and glue sticks. "So, what exactly are we supposed to do?"

Anna had already briefly explained the idea of attraction to her friends. "Well, I've been trying different ways to deliberately focus on attracting what I want into my life. Depending on my mood, I pray or meditate or visualize what I want to come true. I thought it might also be a good idea to pull together pictures to look at periodically. I thought we could essentially create collages."

Pretty soon the kitchen table was littered with paper scraps, opened glue sticks and growing piles of coveted magazine images. Anna paused in her 'work' to take in the scene and feel thankful for the moment: Christmas music was quietly playing; the scent of pine mingled with sweet cocoa; the tree was glittering, and the afternoon sun poured in through the kitchen windows.

"Would you like this one?" Barbara asked Anna, holding out a picture of a lovely Cape Cod style house.

"Sure, thanks." Her friends knew Anna was looking for images involving new homes, land and gardens. She was also picking out pictures of beautiful, slim clothes. Just for the heck of it she included scenes of home offices that appealed to her. Anna had no idea what work she'd do in 'her office,' but she loved the idea of a satisfying, lucrative career she could actually do at home while the girls were in school.

"Oh, look at this!" Charlotte held up a picture of an adorable golden retriever puppy. Her friends smiled. Charlotte never could resist an 'orphaned' face. Charlotte's collage was becoming a mix of an animal shelter and a travel agency brochure. Anna smiled to herself. She never understood how Charlotte survived her marathon vacations with her two young kids. She bet this time Charlotte was envisioning exotic destinations with only David in tow.

Glancing at Barbara's collage, Anna spotted mostly expensive cooking equipment. Barbara loved to cook for her friends and family. Anna never knew how her husband, George, managed to stay trim in light of Barbara's delicious concoctions. Anna, herself, was already anticipating the Christmas cookies Barbara baked each year and gave as presents. (Then she remembered her diet and groaned inwardly. Well, maybe just one or two cookies...) The remainder of Barbara's collage incorporated large, sunny kitchens in which to put her ideal cooking appliances and other odds and ends that most of them had included: new computers, cars and stylish home furnishings.

"You know," Anna said slowly as she flipped through a J.Jill Catalog, "I may do this project with Martha."

"With Martha? Does she know about our club?" Charlotte asked, pausing in her careful extraction of a kitten from a cat food ad.

"I haven't told her about our meetings. But I did talk to her about how her thoughts affect her life."

"Really? What was her reaction?"

"The wonderful thing about Martha's age is that she's still young enough to believe what her mother tells her. Of course, sometimes that worries me, too. I mean, I don't want to lead her down the wrong path. But, listen to this: she began changing her attitude about math, and now she's consistently finishing the quizzes on time and getting mostly A's!"

"Really?"

"Yeah! Well, it makes sense. She used to say things like 'I can never finish all the problems' and 'I hate math quizzes.' Once you announce you can never do something, that's it-- you've made a decision. Even just changing it slightly to 'I can do better' allows for much more possibilities."

"The old 'I think I can' story," Barbara said, sipping her cocoa. "I wonder if my kids would be at all open to any of this. 'Course, Chris is about to enter the teenage angst years. I'll be lucky if he stays open to bathing regularly."

Charlotte laughed. "I know what you mean. I've been considering discussing these new ideas with David, but I'm a little worried about what he'll think."

"Yeah, that's been on my mind a bit, too," Anna agreed. Nibbling on a sinfully buttery cookie and vowing to eat a lighter dinner, she added, "I feel like Adam and I could get so much further so much faster if we tackled life

166

as a team with all these principles in mind. Things like finances and finding and affording our new home involve both of us. In fact, most of that is really about him, at least on the money end of things."

"So, what do you think you'll do?" Barbara asked.

"I don't know. I'm like you," Anna said to Charlotte. "I have no idea what he'd think. I guess I'll just have to see if the right moment comes."

.... As it turned out, the 'right' moment presented itself that very night. The girls had gone to sleep, or at least should have, and Adam and Anna were watching TV. At about 10:30 p.m. Martha came creeping down the stairs.

"What's wrong, sweetie?"

"I can't sleep," Martha looked genuinely upset.

"Did you have a nightmare?" Anna pulled Martha down beside her, wrapping her arms protectively around the small shoulders. Martha seemed younger and more vulnerable at night wearing her footed jammies with her hair all rumpled.

"No, I haven't fallen asleep yet. I've been worrying."

167

"What about?"

"You know how you said what we think about a lot comes true?"

"Ye--e-s."

"I can't seem to stop thinking about that meteor that hit the earth and killed all the dinosaurs. What if I make that happen now?"

It was the tears in Martha's eyes that kept Anna from snorting in laughter. She was just so taken off guard--never in a million years would that have occurred to her. And, yet, it didn't really surprise her that Martha was pondering it. All of her free time was spent reading books, and many of those involved science.

Anna was aware that Adam was looking at them both oddly as she answered, "You don't need to worry about that, Martha. Not every thought we have actually comes true. For one thing, we have time to reconsider what's on our minds and change our thoughts. For another, good thoughts have much more power than bad ones. If you find yourself worrying, just let it go. Or, replace those feelings with peaceful ones about what a beautiful planet we share and how it's here to stay for billions of more years."

168

Martha gave a little smile and snuggled closer to her mother. Her little body began to relax. Anna hoped she'd eased her mind. It must have been awfully stressful worrying you held the fate of all earthly life in your thoughts! Anna felt a little guilty that her teachings had caused Martha so much worry. On the other hand, she was proud and impressed that Martha believed so completely in her influence over her own world. Anna felt it would serve Martha well to know she didn't have to be a victim in all of her 'growing up' stages. Anna knew she certainly could have benefited from some of that knowledge, especially during those emotional adolescent and teenage years.

After a few minutes, Anna walked Martha back upstairs and tucked her in. Feeling a little anxious, she headed back to the living room to face Adam.

"What in the world was that all about?" Adam asked as soon as Anna was settled on her corner of the sofa.

"Remember I told you I was reading Annie McDowell's journal? Well...." She proceeded to generally outline the principles of gratitude, the power of our expectations and even the idea of attraction. She then

169

explained how Martha had been using it to do better in school. Anna studied Adam's face for evidence of amusement or ridicule, but found none. Instead, he looked very thoughtful before saying, "There's actually some scientific evidence of that kind of thing in quantum physics, you know."

"Really?" Anna, of course, did not know. Her strengths in school had been of the language variety, not science.

"Yeah, you know the whole debate over whether the smallest component of matter is a particle or a wave? Well, they've found that the component 'becomes' a particle or a wave based on which the researcher expects to see. In other words, our thoughts seem to be somehow connected to the physical world."

"Wow, that's amazing!"

"Plus, there's the placebo effect--you know, when patients taking sugar pills end up feeling better because they believe they're receiving true medication. You can't deny that our thoughts do have power. It's just not very well understood yet."

"You know, I'm relieved. I was afraid you'd think I'd gone nutty or gotten wrapped up in some weird new age mumbo-jumbo."

"No, but I am a little surprised that you've embraced it all so quickly. I mean, does it go against your Christian background?"

Anna shifted in her seat and thought a moment. "Actually, no. In fact, I think it helps explain a lot. I mean, I think Jesus was referring to it when he performed his miracles. I believe Jesus was indeed performing miracles, but I also think what the person truly expected to happen played a role, too. Jesus would often first ask if the person truly believed, and if the person did, then he'd say 'Get up and walk.' It always came down to belief, faith and conviction."

"But if you can create your own experience, where does God fit in?"

"First of all, God gave us minds to think with! Secondly, I believe we hold the belief and conviction, but God actually brings it about. It's a co-operative effort, if you will. I don't think we could have any power in our lives without a God-force behind it all."

Adam nodded slowly.

"I see God as a loving, supportive creator who always intended for man to have a glorious experience here on Earth. I think it's man who got it all muddled and under-valued his abilities."

"Sounds like a typical man," Adam said, grinning.

"Well, anyway, I'm glad I can talk to you about it," Anna said, feeling that they'd probably covered enough ground for tonight. Some other time she'd introduce the idea of how to use these principles in their family goals....like a new home!

CHAPTER SEVEN

"How was yesterday?" Faith asked.

"It was good. The girls were happy. I'm just a bit pooped, though," Anna said. She actually felt like she had a Christmas hangover, minus the alcohol--simply too much shopping, baking, wrapping, caroling and visiting. She'd eaten more than she intended, too, and was uncomfortably aware of the waistband in the size 14 jeans she'd been so proud to fit into. 'Ho-ho-freakin-ho' she thought. Perhaps because she threw herself so freely into the holiday season, by December 26th she was more than ready to pack it in.

"Do you know we had essentially three Christmases yesterday?" It made Anna tired all over again just thinking about it. "I mean, first we opened Santa's presents at home, then drove to Adam's parents' house and exchanged presents there, and finally finished at Mom's last night for a third celebration!"

Faith looked concerned. "I guess that's what we'll have to look forward to next year," she groaned, unconsciously holding her very pregnant, protruding tummy.

173

"Oh, no, I'm sorry. It'll be fun! Little whoever will be crawling everywhere and maybe even taking steps. And everyone will have so much fun shopping for baby toys again," Anna said, remembering the magic of her daughters' first Christmases. Faith smiled, looking more optimistic. It sometimes struck Anna as odd, looking into a face that was almost an exact mirror of her own. Out in public together they often still got second glances from people who hesitantly asked if they were sisters. Of course, there were differences. Faith's blonde hair was permed, and she tended to wear less make-up than Anna. And, obviously, Faith was now eight months pregnant.

The sisters' time together was always therapeutic for both of them. There truly was a twin bond that couldn't be explained or ignored. Their close relationship with their mother and even with their respective husbands could never rival the one they shared together. Without being fully conscious of it, Anna was a tiny bit jealous of Faith's unborn baby. A little part of her feared that once Faith had a child, she wouldn't have as much room for her twin. She didn't allow herself to consciously dwell on that thought for long.

174

Instead, she took a second to be thankful for the moment. She and Faith were sitting at a table in Barnes and Noble, one of their favorite meeting spots in Richmond. Usually they spent more time roaming the store, but these days Faith preferred to sit as much as possible. So, having escaped for some time to themselves, the sisters sipped their peppermint hot cocoa and indulged in some serious girl talk.

"It seems like forever ago now, but you said something about reading Granny's journal and meeting with your friends. Did anything ever come of that?" Faith asked.

Anna laughed. "Yeah, we're the Enlightened Ladies Club."

"What?""

"I know, it sounds silly, but we meet every week or two and figured we may as well give ourselves a name."

"So, what do you do in your club?"

Anna proceeded to tell Faith as succinctly as possible about the power behind our thoughts, about attraction and the purpose of our feelings.

"So, we try to put these ideas into practice and compare how it goes," Anna concluded.

Faith looked distracted. "I could use some of that power." She fiddled with her now empty cup, looking worried. "I don't know how we're going to make things work once the baby comes." Anna looked sympathetically at her sister. They shared the same smoky blue eyes, except Faith's now held an expression of worry and distress. Anna knew her sister would give anything to work part-time. But, with her Master's degree, she earned more than Matt and had carried them both on her insurance. She and Matt had just moved into their first home, and they'd have day care to pay for once Faith's maternity leave ran out.

"Well, Faith, I don't know how it would all work out, but I think you should still hold onto your dream of staying home part-time with the baby"

"But, I don't see how.." Faith's eyes shone brightly with tears before she blinked them away.

"I know, but that's okay. It's up to God to work out the 'how' part. Let yourself think about it, visualize it, and get excited about it." Faith looked guardedly hopeful, so Anna continued, "More than anything, I want a new

176

home with land and privacy, and I want a wonderful career of my own. Now, I have no idea how to make those things happen. I just know that it's always on my mind. But, dwelling on how unhappy I am about not having it yet will get me nowhere. So, I've begun thinking about how it would feel if I did have it. I look at magazines; I picture it in my head; I try to get really excited about it now, even before it's a reality. I believe by doing all of that, I'm attracting it into my life. I have no idea how, but that doesn't matter, 'cause that's God's part."

"And you really think it will work out?"

"Yeah, I really do."

Faith sighed. "I'd like to believe that, but..." Her voice trailed off.

"Well, just give it a try. It can't hurt anything. Have fun with it. I think the idea is to first change the way you feel. When you think of working part-time, I bet you actually feel depressed, right?" Faith nodded. "That's because you're painfully aware of not having what you want. I'd been feeling the same way about moving and working. If you let yourself daydream about it without trying to work out the 'how' details, you start to

177

feel better. To attract what you want into your life, you first have to feel good about it. Once the thought of working part-time actually feels good and exciting, instead of depressing, it becomes so much more possible! Do you see?"

"I think so," Faith said slowly.

"I know, it's a different way of looking at things."

"Yeah, but I'm open to anything at this point. I'm just so tired of feeling stuck, trapped."

"Well, what would working part-time mean to you? Can you think of some concrete ways it would change things?"

Faith stared off into space, absently rubbing her swollen tummy.

"Hmmmm...I guess I'd be able to cook some yummier dinners. I'd have a little more time to paint the upstairs. Those white walls are getting on my nerves! Obviously, I'd have more time with the baby. I could read him or her lots of books and we could go out to parks and go window shopping together."

"Come on," Anna said, suddenly helping Faith to her feet.

178

"Where are we going?"

Anna proceeded to slowly lead her sister around the store, gathering magazines and books as they went. Twenty minutes later they were once again seated at a table, pouring over their treasures. They perused children's books they loved and hadn't looked at in years. Faith began a mental list of all the books she'd like to obtain to read to the baby. They looked through cookbooks, finding some very delicious and do-able recipes. They also gazed at magazine photos, searching for the color combination Faith would like to paint the upstairs rooms. After a very enjoyable hour, Faith felt immeasurably better. She ended up purchasing a book of the classic Winnie the Pooh stories, a crock pot cookbook and a decorating magazine. She and Anna vowed to remind each other of their dreams and help keep their expectations alive. Faith had become an honorary member of the Enlightened Ladies Club!

.... Anna never remembered being as thrilled on New Year's Day as she was on this New Year's. To her it was generally a sort-of nothing day, filled with vague nagging feelings that she should be doing something notable to start the new year on the right foot. The main

179

reason for her euphoria this time was the knowledge that school began again tomorrow. Martha and Lucy had endured way too much time together these past two weeks, and Anna had endured all she could of them. Adam had been able to escape the worst of it by returning to work right after Christmas. Anna was sure she noticed a spring in his step as he practically whistled 'heigh-ho, off to work I go' on his way out the door each morning. Anna, on the other hand, was trapped in the townhouse with two cats, one dog, and two kids--all bored, stir crazy and taking it out on each other. At the end of one such day it was with a touch of petty satisfaction that Anna watched Adam running into the house, stripping as he went, yelling, "Scabies!" this time as he rushed to a scalding shower.

Anna had taken down the Christmas tree, unpacked from their jaunt to Richmond, generally straightened up and somehow found places to put away the girls' new toys. She was hoping New Year's Day could therefore be relatively chore-free. She also had hopes that the girls would be lethargic, considering they'd stayed up to ring in the new year. Anna and Adam had never been big on partying, so they had developed their own tradition: they created an indoor picnic complete with blanket, champagne and finger food. They then watched the ball drop in Times Square from the cozy comfort of their living room floor. After having kids, they continued the tradition. It had only been the last year or two that the girls were finally old enough to make it until midnight and join their parents' picnic. To stay awake, Martha insisted on hours of board games. By 12:01 a.m. they were all ready to call it a night. If Anna had to endure one more game of Sorry, she wouldn't be responsible for her actions.

It seemed, though, rather than leaving the girls quiet and subdued, the late night had only caused magnified crankiness. If they tried to play together, they argued. If they weren't arguing, they were absently following Anna around the house. After telling them three times to go find something to do, Anna finally closed her library book and sat it down. Both girls were simply sitting and staring at her. For the umpteenth time she wondered where Adam had disappeared to. How could he manage to stay hidden in a 1500 square foot townhouse? She could never get away with trying to slip unnoticed into another room. Sometimes she felt like one

181

of those tagged animals in the wild. Her every moment was tracked by a blip on a radar screen. 'Where's Mom? Oh, look, the little blinking light is headed to the bedroom. Let's go see what she's doing!'

With a resigned sigh, she suggested, "Do you guys want to do some crafts?"

"Yay!" the girls cheered. Anna soon had the table once again covered by card stock, glue sticks, scissors, cocoa, cookies and magazines. This time, though, she included toy catalogues they'd been inundated with in the weeks before Christmas.

"What is I'm doing?" Lucy asked, with a cookie in one hand and a pair of scissors in the other. Anna smiled. She'd miss it when Lucy's funny little grammatical hiccups disappeared.

"Are we making collages?" Martha asked, her eyes already skimming the delicious toy catalogs.

"Yes, exactly."

"Colleges?" Lucy asked.

"No, collages. It's like a little poster filled with pictures. The idea with this one is I want you all to glue down pictures of what you'd love to have in our house," Anna explained.

182

"New house? Are we moving?" Martha asked.

"Well, not yet, but we'd like to in another year or so. Remember how our thoughts eventually create things? I think we should go ahead and be planning what we want to see in our new home and yard."

Martha looked a little unsure as how to begin.

"Think about your new bedroom. What would you like in it? Maybe a desk? Bunk beds?" Anna tried to get them inspired.

"A couch!" Lucy said.

"Well..."

"Um..."

"My own TV!" Lucy shouted.

Anna's first motherly reaction was to tell her girls not to be so materialistic. But then she thought, 'Oh, why the heck not? Why not shoot for the stars?' If she began telling her daughters that they couldn't afford things or should feel wrong for wanting things, they would grow up believing it. There was nothing wrong in enjoying the good things in life. As long as you were taught to appreciate your blessings and to be generous toward others, there was nothing inherently evil in having possessions. There was also certainly no virtue in poverty

183

and destitution. It was a new way of thinking for Anna, but she was beginning to feel that God intended for people to be wealthy in all areas--good health, family and friends, spiritually and even monetarily. She used to feel that wealth was a matter of the 'haves' and the 'have nots.' You were pretty much born into one group or the other, unless you invented something phenomenal or became a world famous actor or athlete, you stayed a 'have not.'

Now, though, she was finally understanding that wealth and abundance are first and foremost a state of mind. She never let herself consider it before, but gosh darn it, Anna did want to be monetarily wealthy. She wanted for her and Adam to be financially secure and never a burden to their children. She wanted them to be able to pay for improvements in her mother's home and help both their sets of parents live in dignity and comfort through their old age. She wanted to take the girls on memorable vacations now and still be able to help them get on their feet in their early adulthood. She wanted to be able to help out friends and family when they were struggling. And, she wanted a certain ease of living--not dreading the next mortgage payment, not panicking when a large car repair was needed, not limiting when they

184

could actually go out to eat or see a movie. Her whole life had been spent in this way: sort-of rationing out how much 'living' could be done at any one time. And, it was all struggle based on a strong awareness of and belief in lack over abundance. Well, Anna was sick of it! And she certainly didn't want to set her girls up for the same struggles.

So, going against her instincts, Anna smiled and nodded when the girls carefully cut out pictures of electronics, trampolines and even ponies. She began to join in as well, deliberately choosing things that were fantastically frivolous. She cut out a beautiful porcelain doll from FAO Schwartz, a diamond tennis bracelet from Kay Jewelers and a leather tote bag from Coldwater Creek. Remembering the new home, she also found some beautiful furnishings in Crate and Barrel and Pottery Barn catalogs. Flipping through Better Homes and Gardens, Anna spotted a medicine ad that read 'Listen to Your Mother'. She cut it out and slipped it on top of Martha's stack of pictures. The next time Martha went to add to the pile, she stopped short. "What's this?" she laughed, looking at Anna. Pretty soon they were all having as much fun finding silly phrases and pictures to thrust upon one another as actually making collages.

Martha, of course, got the idea and found as many Pepto Bismol-type of ads as possible, and ones for kitty litter--anything that seemed a bit rude or gross. Lucy, however, had no idea what was going on, but was determined to join in the hilarity. Anna became almost hysterically giggly as she received random pictures and words: a Campbell's soup ad; THE; a vase of flowers, Purina dog food, OF...Adam crept into the kitchen, expecting to hear bickering. Instead, he found his three ladies laughing uproariously and pitching bits of paper at one another. He shook his head piteously. 'They've truly lost it,' he thought. 'Well, it was inevitable.' He quietly slipped back downstairs.

.... The Enlightened Ladies sat together once again at the coffee shop, looking a bit war weary and shell shocked. They had each survived the chaos of Christmas and the subsequent week of up close and personal time with their kids. Charlotte, of course, was used to having her kids at home all the time, but this past week she'd endured them, plus half a dozen new toys that buzzed,

186

talked and beeped. The women were in need of some serious peace and quiet.

Therefore, outside of the normal pleasantries, they simply sat in silence for an unusually long time, enjoying their coffee. It was Charlotte who eventually spoke, "So, did either of you make any New Year's resolutions?"

"I always have my old standby one to lose weight and get in shape." Barbara took a bit of her chocolate muffin, adding, "'Course, that's been my resolution for the past five years, so I'm not that uptight about it."

Charlotte and Anna laughed. "Well, I didn't even make one," Charlotte confessed. "Somehow for me it's always doomed from the start. Simply because I've set a goal, a part of me immediately starts figuring ways to sabotage it; you know, like a child ignoring good advice just because it was her mother who suggested it."

""Then maybe you should set a goal opposite of what you really want, like 'I'm going to get no exercise all year," Barbara joked.

"I usually go for the losing weight one, myself," Anna said.

187

"You look like you've already lost some," Charlotte pointed out.

"Yeah, I noticed that, too, and I hated you for it," Barbara said, grinning. "No, really, that's great."

"Thanks. I've been working on it, but Christmas-time was hard. Anyway, this year I thought I'd make a more general resolution. I decided to make an effort to consistently use these new ideas we've talked about. I'm going to try and really work on attracting good changes into my life, mainly weight loss, better finances and a new house." Anna ticked off each one with her fingers.

"But that sounds more like work than dieting and exercising!" Barbara said.

"Not really. It basically boils down to two things: focus only on what I want in life and go ahead and be happy about it now."

"You think it's really that simple?"

"Well, it's got to make some sort of difference. It's certainly a far cry from how I looked at my life most of last year."

"What about having your own career, too? I remember all those home offices you put in your collage," Barbara said.

188

Anna hesitated. "Oh, yeah..." She felt a little more certain about her other goals. She'd conveniently overlooked her career plans because they seemed even more far-fetched than buying her dream home. "Well, I don't know. I mean, I still want a career. I guess I'm just having trouble getting a clear picture in my head of what I'd be doing."

""Think about it, Anna. If you didn't have to work out any of the details, what would you just love to do?"

Feeling a little put on the spot, Anna tried to brainstorm. Before she could come up with an answer, Barbara interjected, "I know what I'd love."

"Yeah, go ahead," Anna encouraged. She felt she needed some inspiration.

"I'd love to do something with cooking. I wouldn't want to work in a restaurant, but I'd love to cook in my spare time and actually make money from it."

"What about catering?"

"Hm...I'm not sure. It sounds awfully ambitious. I wouldn't want jittery brides-to-be and their mothers nit-picking everything I offered."

"Writing!" Anna suddenly blurted out.

189

"What?"

"That's what I'd love to do--be a children's author."

"Really?"

"Yeah. I was always good at writing in high school and college. Of course, most of that wasn't creative writing, but, still, I enjoyed it.

"What made you think of kids' books?"

"Well, Martha's begun reading Beverly Cleary and Judy Blume lately. It's made me remember how much I loved all those classics. I don't think I'd be good at the truly fanciful things, like Madeleine L'Engle's books. But, a lot of the others are pretty much about family life. I hadn't really put a lot of stock in it, but I've found myself noticing funny things the girls say or do lately and thinking 'that would make a good story.'"

"That sounds fun! You should do it!" Charlotte said.

"What, for real? I'm not sure..."

"Why not?"

"Well, what about you?" Anna turned the tables on her friend. "What would you do?"

"You should do something with animals," Barbara advised, "You know, put your love of strays to work for you somehow."

Charlotte's eyes lit up but then looked wary. "David would kill me if I brought any more homeless animals into our house."

"You wouldn't have to bring animals home. Maybe you could help out an animal shelter or something."

While her friends discussed Charlotte's options, Anna couldn't help but let her mind mull over the book idea. Could she really do it? Was she good enough? She knew she was talented with things like critical essays, but creative writing? This idea was crazy...and yet.....

"....so, I think we should go for it," Charlotte was saying.

"Sorry, what?" Anna realized her friend was talking to her.

"Let's make a pact to each go after a goal!" Barbara and Anna looked at their friend skeptically. "I'm serious!" Charlotte insisted, "The whole point about remembering gratitude and working on our thoughts has been to make our lives better, right? So, let's really do it, go after something specific."

"Why do I feel like I'm being double dared?" Barbara asked. Anna giggled nervously, but she was intrigued.

"This coming week let's each try and come up with a specific goal we'd love to see come true. I triple dare you!" Charlotte laughed.

"You're on!" Barbara said.

"For now, don't worry about details, just try to put in one clear sentence what your dream is," Anna suggested.

.... Anna would later regret her 'one clear sentence' idea. It wasn't as easy as it seemed. Narrowing it to a sentence meant having to be very clear in her head about exactly what she wanted to see come true. She also found it difficult not to let the 'how' details interfere with her dreams. In other words, every time she went to form her sentence she'd end up getting distracted by questions of how to make it work. As soon as she started down that path, though, all of her lofty goals fell apart before she'd even begun them.

192

"Okay," Anna finally said to herself, "The 'what' of my goal is up to me; the 'how' is up to God." Keeping that in mind, the exercise became fun once again...That is, it was fun until Anna decided to share her goal with Adam.

"And so, here's my sentence," Anna said, having finished explaining her friend's idea, "'I am becoming a successfully published children's author, with book signings and contracts lined up well into the future.' What do you think?"

There was a momentary hesitation before Adam asked, "You want to write kids' books?"

"Yeah. I know I don't have a background in creative writing, but I've certainly got plenty of inspiration!"

"Okay, well, sure, go ahead." Adam didn't sound like he was brimming with enthusiasm.

"What's wrong?" Anna suddenly felt leaden. "You don't mind me trying it, do you?"

"No, of course not. It's just, I'd imagine publishing is pretty cut-throat. I don't want you to be disappointed. I mean, it can take quite awhile to get published, you know."

"I know that, Adam. I don't have stars in my eyes. I'm not expecting overnight fame. I just thought it would be something fun to work on while Lucy's still little and my options are limited." Anna realized she was reducing her goal to more of a hobby for Adam's benefit.

"Okay, sweetie, sounds good, really. I didn't mean to criticize. I'd love to read your writing."

.... After Adam had left the room, Anna mumbled, "Over my dead body." She had no intention of sharing any of her writing attempts with him. She was furious. She knew part of her anger was based on fear; in many ways Adam was just voicing the same doubts Anna herself felt. But a large part of her anger stemmed from deep disappointment. She so wanted Adam to believe in her and truly support her. Anna didn't want to feel patronized, or that her husband was humoring her, as he would if Martha said she wanted to set up a lemonade stand. Anna smiled bitterly. It seemed Adam was supportive as long as her writing idea remained a hobby, something harmless to keep her occupied until both girls were in school and she could maybe get a 'real' job. She knew she wasn't being entirely fair to her husband, but

194

she was hurt. Right then, to herself, she vowed to become a successful author. This would not be a hobby, damn it; it would be a lucrative career.

.... Two days later Anna set out for the bookstore on a mission. She was determined to find the secret of penetrating the publishing world. Two hours later she was practically in tears. She'd perused every publication from writer's magazines to entire encyclopedia-sized volumes on publishing guidelines and everything in between. Her brain had turned to jelly, and she felt even more lost than she had been earlier that morning. At least then she'd been happily ignorant. What did she think she was doing? This wasn't some happy-go-lucky project she was undertaking; from everything she'd seen so far it was all out war! 'Maybe Adam's right,' Anna thought, 'maybe this business is too hard for me. I don't even understand half of what's in these books!' Momentarily ignoring her diet, she bought a cafe mocha to go and headed for some comfort; in the time remaining before having to collect Lucy, Anna would read more of Annie McDowell's writings.

195

.... Anna was seated on the couch under a cozy blanket, surrounded by her two sleeping cats. Glancing at the clock, she figured she had a little over an hour before she needed to walk Max and pick up Lucy. She sent up a silent prayer as she opened the folder containing her grandmother's essays. She felt she needed some true inspiration to keep her from sinking into complete discouragement. Intrigued by the title, Anna picked up one and began reading...

Acting 'As If'

I use a variety of techniques to help me when I need a boost. Sometimes I just need to get a little perspective on life--just step back and see that life is basically good and everything is fine. Sometimes it's much more dramatic--I'm feeling very low, panicked, and fearful and need to be brought back from the edge of the cliff. One way I try to get back on track is 'acting as if.' For example, let's say my current fear is about lack of money. My habitual reaction to extremely low finances is fear and panic. Even if I'm trying to trust God, I find myself feeling anxious and trying to work out solutions in my head. I feel I can't even leave the house, hardly, because it's hard to go out and spend not a penny, if only for gas. I immediately begin figuring how I can stretch our food, to make halfway decent dinners and pack lunches that aren't completely mismatched. In other words, I go into 'lack' mode, 'survival' mode. Clearly, I'm not trusting God. How can I be truly trusting and still feeling it's up to me to somehow make it all work, make resources stretch? But, at the same time, how realistic is it for me to simply go from worry to complete peace in an instant--like hitting a light switch? I suppose if my faith were strong enough, then I could. For now, though, it's difficult for me to so easily and completely feel different. What is easier, though, is to begin acting different first. I've found that once I change my actions, my feelings begin to change to match them. For example, I may be feeling lazy and maybe even a little down, dreading the idea of getting up and doing housework. Still, I make myself stand up, begin gathering laundry, run the vacuum, etc. Initially I still feel slow and maybe aggravated about all the work to do. Gradually, though, as I bustle about, I begin to feel my energy increasing. Also, as I begin completing tasks and see how nice the carpet looks and how the coffee table gleams with polish,

197

my 'low' feelings begin to lift to ones of pleasure, accomplishment and even happiness. In this case, I made myself get up and begin 'acting as if' I was filled with energy and purpose to get the house beautiful.

Back to the money fears, one of the most effective ways for me to move from panic to peace is 'acting as if.' In this case, it's acting as if we have plenty of money for all of our family's needs; acting as if we had an endless bank account; acting as if God Himself were at my side, handing me cash for everything I need....whatever image is most salient for me. Then, I begin acting that way. Now, that doesn't mean I do anything foolhardy like write a check for a new dining room table that we can't afford or charge a new diamond ring on a credit card. Instead, I take small positive actions to counteract the 'survival' mode mentality. I may go and buy a small bouquet of flowers and put them in a simple glass vase in a prominent place in my house. Instead of wallowing in deprivation, I lavishly use and enjoy all the 'riches' I already possess: I light candles, play music, soak in a bubble bath, fix a pot of tea or check out an armload of library books. With confidence that God will replenish the supply, I take the best of all we have from the pantry and freezer and enjoy preparing a nice dinner for the family. Just like with cleaning the house, taking these positive actions begins to change my feelings. I feel a bit more abundant, a little more confident, and more peaceful--which puts me in a calmer state of mind to begin accepting God's grace and experiencing true trust.

I know it may sound overly simplistic , but it really does work. Sometimes, when I've been at my very lowest--times in my life when I've been truly depressed, feeling despair, whatever the cause, I would tell myself to 'act as if' there were no tomorrow. It may sound trite, but think for a moment if today truly were your last day on Earth and you knew it. There would certainly be no point in worrying about finances, holding grudges or wasting time with self-pity. What would you want to do with your time? Suddenly your focus would be shifted to what's really important: engaging your children in play without being distracted, or looking into your husband's eyes and sharing a first date type of kiss. You'd also take time to notice and enjoy life's simple pleasures, like fragrant flowers, clean clothes, brewing coffee, hot showers and music that speaks to your soul. I know we've all heard the advice of 'stop and smell the roses.' It's just that when I'm

199

weighted down with life, 'acting as if' today is all I have helps me to lighten up. I'm the type of person who tends to take things seriously. I sometimes need to remind myself that God means for us to enjoy life and live it fully, not perfectly.

'Acting as if' works because it shifts your focus from what you don't want to what you do want. Where you focus, where you're putting all of your energy, is where you're headed. When I'm focused on lack and putting my energy into 'survival' mode. I'm heading deeper into the world of deprivation. When I'm focused on lack of energy and dread about household chores, those chores seem to grow bigger and more impossible to complete. The same is true with any area of life-- relationships, health, the workplace, etc. Try 'acting as if' and see how it changes your perspective and even your feelings.

Anna put down the folder and stretched. 'Acting as if' was an interesting concept. She wondered how she could use it to help her writing endeavors. She stood up and called Max. Snapping on his leash and heading out the door, Anna pondered the fact that it all seemed to

200

come back to feelings. The main idea seemed to be to do whatever it took to raise your spirits.

Anna all but ran from one townhouse to the next, being dragged along by Max. As always, she tried to avoid fixating on the houses that were unkempt or always seemed to have people loitering around in the middle of the day. She had been trying to make it a habit in all areas of her life not to put focus and energy on the things that made her unhappy or irritated. Because, once you felt good about something, you would begin attracting more of the good to you, and the same was true of the opposite! Annie McDowell's examples had been about money and housework. How could Anna 'act as if' to improve her feelings about writing a book? She paused to let Max sniff eagerly all around his favorite lamppost before claiming it as his territory, as he did every day. Right now she felt overwhelmed, discouraged and pessimistic. She wanted to feel excited, optimistic and confident. Almost more than those, though, she wanted to feel light hearted. She realized the book idea had been fun when she hadn't been so serious about it. To prove herself to Adam, she'd rushed off to the bookstore to figure out how to get published. She'd dropped the 'fun' part and rushed headlong into the details.

Having quickly circled back to her townhouse, Anna let Max inside and grabbed her purse. As she made the familiar journey to Lucy's preschool, Anna decided it was time to take a different approach to her writing project. What if she 'acted as if' she already had a publisher committed to making her book? What if she 'acted as if' she had a wonderful agent who was guaranteed to get her profitable contracts and make her book a success? Then, she could simply enjoy the process of writing and feel relaxed about the details.

Anna arrived at Lucy's preschool a few minutes early. Sitting in her car, she pulled out a pen and a deposit slip. Out of habit, she glanced at the pen: 'Zyrtec' this time. Almost all of her pens came from drug reps who visited Adam's office. She was glad of the free pens. She just hoped one day she wouldn't pull a 'Viagra' one out to write a check at Wal-Mart. Anna began making a list on the back of the slip:

To do:

- clean out area around computer table
- buy pens and small notebook for purse

202

- set up writing schedule on MWF
- get printer paper
- to library to get kids' books to re-read
- buy new ink cartridge

She still felt unsure about this new venture, but she certainly wasn't despairing like she had been that morning.

Anna locked up the car and headed into the school to collect Lucy. Moments later, her little one filed into the lobby, along with a string of pint-sized pupils. They all struggled under the weight of their winter coats, backpacks and lunch boxes. Anna chatted a minute with Lucy's teacher before relieving Lucy of her load and heading for the car.

Once Lucy was safely strapped in and they were on the road, Anna asked tentatively, "How was your day? What did you do?"

"Grandparent's Day is soon."

"Oh."

"We're 'posed to bring our grandparents to school and sing to them."

"Hmmmm…" Anna knew none of Lucy's grandparents would be able to attend. They all either still

203

worked full time or were too far away. Anna's mom was the only retired one, but she was in Arkansas visiting her sister for two weeks. "Um, Lucy, I don't think any of your grandparents can come."

"Yes they can! It's Grandparent's day!"

"But, see, Grandma and Grandpa will be at work and Granny is far away seeing her sister. Granddad lives in Ohio."

"Mommy, my teacher said they could come."

"Yes, I know they're allowed to come. What I mean is that they probably can't."

"Yes they can! IT'S GRANDPARENT'S DAY!"

Anna felt like beating her head against the steering wheel. How did she and Lucy always end up in these ridiculous 'who's on first' type of arguments? And it always seemed to happen on the drive home from preschool. Anna just let this one drop, hoping Lucy would forget about Grandparent's Day. Anna would write a note to Lucy's teacher and explain it all. Maybe Mrs. Chase could get Lucy to understand and not be too disappointed.

.... For Anna, a trip to the office supply store was as yummy as perusing a candy shop. Perhaps because she'd

204

never had to use the materials for an actual business, it was like playing 'grown-up.' Martha felt the same way. She had more pencils, sticky notes and erasers in her bedroom than she'd ever use in a lifetime. Anna had considered taking Martha along on her office supply outing, and then she reconsidered. As much as she'd enjoy treating her daughter, she knew the trip would become mostly about Martha, and Anna would end up rushing through her own choices. So, going against her initial instincts, she tactfully refrained from mentioning it and decided to go while both girls were in school. Boy it was amazing how ingrained it was for Anna to always put her kids first! She truly had to make an effort to do something only for herself.

Feeling almost devious, Anna headed straight for Staples after her workout. She took her time walking up and down each aisle, even the ones containing things she had no need for, like briefcases and packing supplies. Finally getting down to work, she stopped in front of a wall of pens. After careful consideration, Anna chose a package of black medium gel pens. She then wandered about the store. She found a tiny notebook to keep in her purse for any random ideas she'd want to jot down at

205

inopportune moments. She also bought legal pads and splurged on a leather folder that would hold a legal pad and pen. Anna figured at first she'd compose long-hand. Somehow that seemed like less pressure than sitting in front of a blank computer screen. Just in case, though, she did get some printer paper and an extra ink cartridge.

Anna hurried out to the car with her purchases, having only just remembered that today was a half day at Lucy's school. Knowing Lucy would only have had a snack, Anna decided to take her out for a treat: lunch at Burger King (or Booger King, as Lucy would say) where they had a ball pit to play in. She figured while Lucy played she could maybe begin some brainstorming about book ideas.

"So, sweetie, how was your school morning?" Anna asked, glancing in the rearview mirror at her little one. Lucy's tiny face appeared even more elfin, because, for once, she let Anna braid her hair into long thin pigtails. Also, for once, Lucy had actually left the braids in place.

"Andrew fell asleep in class today."

"Really? What were you all doing when he fell asleep?"

206

"We were laughing!"

"Oh," Anna smiled. She turned into the fast food parking lot and pulled out her new leather folder and legal pad.

A few minutes later she and Lucy were settled at a booth next to the play area, Anna with her salad and Lucy with her chicken strips kid's meal. It had taken all of Anna's will power not to order her own portion of the oh-so-tasty fries, onion rings or even a cheeseburger. She kept imagining herself bathing suit shopping this spring. The image of her reflection in the changing room mirror under the merciless fluorescent lights--yep, that usually curbed her temptations.

Munching on a french fry, Lucy asked, "What are you doin' with that notebook?"

After Adam's lukewarm reaction, Anna was leery of sharing her writing goals with anyone else. On the other hand, she had hoped the girls would help give her ideas and suggestions.

"Well, I'm going to write a kid's book. Do you have any ideas for it?"

Lucy thought a moment. "I can tell you how to do a book," she stated with confidence.

207

"Really? Great! How?"

With a very serious expression, Lucy announced, "You take a bunch of papers and you staple them together."

"Ah," Anna nodded, trying not to giggle.

"Can I play now, Mommy?"

"Sure." She watched as Lucy leaped into what looked like a gigantic bowl of Trix cereal. While Lucy happily 'swam' among the multicolored balls, Anna pulled out her legal pad and fished a 'Celebrex' pen out of her purse. She'd forgotten and left the package of new pens in the car.

Suddenly it was the moment of truth: pen in hand, poised over a blank sheet of paper. Now what? This was the point Anna had been unconsciously dreading. 'Okay, okay,' she thought, 'write about what you know. So, what do I know about?' She began a list: being a twin; sisters; daughters; Girl Scouts; swimming and gymnastics lessons; motherhood; pets; decorating; cooking; marriage; moving; life in the suburbs; living in Virginia; growing up with divorced parents; Christianity; some arts and crafts, and college. Anna sat back and looked at her list. She felt she should start on a small

208

scale to get her feet wet. Maybe she could write a short story that could become something bigger later.

Anna put her notebook aside in order to finish her salad and think over what short story she could begin with. She speared a cucumber slice and watched Lucy travel down the sliding board into the ball pit. What about a story involving a ball pit that magically turns into a giant's bowl of cereal? Or, a ball pit in which children slip down and through to another enchanted land of some sort? Anna chuckled to herself. She'd have kids terrified to ever jump into another ball pit. Maybe she should wait on the fanciful things--the obvious inspiration was right in front of her, Martha and Lucy. Why not just take something they'd actually done and write about it? It would be a good way to practice setting scenes, including details and developing characters. Trading her fork for a pen, Anna made a second list of family anecdotes: Martha cutting Lucy's hair; Lucy jumping into the pool at age three and being saved by the lifeguard; the girls losing their pet hamster somewhere in the basement, and sister issues of rivalry, arguments and loving moments.

"Mommy, I'm tired of the ball pit," Lucy appeared at Anna's elbow with rumpled clothes and one braid undone.

"Alright. Do you want to go home and pull out some toys?"

"'Kay!"

....   While Martha sat at the table finishing her homework, Anna stood at the kitchen counter with tears streaming down her face. She was chopping onions to go in her ham and bean soup for dinner

"Are you okay, Momma?" Martha looked worried.

"Yeah, sweetie," Anna laughed, "it's just the onions making my eyes water."

"I don't like onions."

"You won't even notice them." Anna loved this simple meal. She made a thick soup of navy and pinto beans and added onions, ham and celery. She seasoned it with pepper and worcestershire and served it with crusty bread. Anna was relieved to scrape the onion pieces into the pot and wash her hands.

"Anyway, Martha, I was saying that I'm going to start practicing writing kid's stories, and I thought I'd

210

begin with the time you cut Lucy's hair. Do you remember that?"

Martha snorted, "I sure do! You and Dad were really mad at me!"

"Yes, well, you did chop a huge chunk out of her hair! It came as a bit of a shock." Mother and daughter laughed together as they reminisced.

"She wanted to play hairdressers. We were having fun! Then you had to take her to the real beauty salon," Martha remembered.

"And they gave her such an adorable little pixie cut that you ended up wanting yours cut, too!"

"So, it all turned out okay," Martha laughed. "Are all your stories going to be about me and Lucy?"

"I don't know. I just thought it would be easier to start with things that had really happened. Maybe later I'll feel more comfortable making things up."

"Can I read them when you're done?"

"I'd love for you to. In fact, since I'm aiming for your age group, I really do need your help. You'll need to tell me what's funny and what isn't, and if the vocabulary is too easy or too hard, things like that."

"Great! When can we start?"

211

"Well, I haven't even written anything yet! I'll let you know when the first draft is done, okay?"

"This is cool! We'll be partners! Just think, your books could end up in our school library! My teacher could read them to the class! My mom could be famous!"

"Hold on, dear," Anna said, feeling alarmed, "don't get carried away. I've just started this whole idea." Martha's face continued to beam, though, and she had a faraway look on her face as she gathered her homework papers and left the room.

"Uh-oh," Anna thought.

CHAPTER EIGHT

"We think she ate her babies," Charlotte was saying as Anna joined her and Barbara at 'their' table.

"What?" Anna asked, setting her coffee and bagel on the table.

"I was telling Barbara that our guinea pig had her babies. We didn't even know she was pregnant! Anyway, apparently she ate them last night."

"How do you know?"

"You don't want to know," Charlotte answered grimly.

"Ugh," Barbra was trying to hide her look of disgust.

"It sounds like Animal Planet come to life over at your house," Anna commented, remembering Charlotte's tale a couple of months ago of their Persian fishing Charlie's beta out of the fish bowl and eating it. Finding the bowl empty, poor little Charles had been afraid he'd get in trouble for 'losing' his fish.

"How did you explain it to Charles?" Anna asked tentatively.

213

Charlotte sighed, "He was the one who discovered it, or them...My son's going to be scarred for life. I can already hear him telling his therapist, 'And then there was the pivotal day I realized that mothers eat their young'..."

Anna and Barbara laughed.

"Maybe Charles will look at you with newfound respect!" Barbara said.

"I guess I'll have to stop telling him that he's so cute I could eat him up," Charlotte said. All three women had a fit of the giggles.

Wiping her streaming eyes, Anna asked, "Well, speaking of animals, did you come up with a sentence for your goal, Charlotte?"

"It was really hard. I mean, even when Charles goes to school in the fall, Emma will still be home with me, so my options are a bit limited. In the end I just said, 'I will devote one day a week to help an animal shelter in some rewarding capacity.'"

"That sounds good," Anna said thoughtfully, "but, unless you mean to keep it in the future, I'd change 'I will' to 'I am beginning to devote.' Have you contacted any shelters yet?"

214

"Yeah, I'm supposed to go visit a couple of them next week. They wanted to show me around the place and explain how they work."

"What has David thought of it?" Barbara asked.

"He was pretty hesitant. I think he envisioned herds of strays moving through our home. As long as I don't add to our current pet roster, I think he'll be supportive." Charlotte took a sip of her coffee before asking Anna, "How about you? What's your sentence?"

Anna recited, "I am becoming a successfully published children's author with book signings and contracts lined up well into the future."

"Wow! That's ambitious!" Barbara said around a mouthful of muffin.

"Yeah, I know, but that would be the ultimate dream."

"So, have you begun taking steps?" Charlotte asked.

"I bought some writing supplies, and I've started brainstorming," Anna told them of her plan to write short stories about anecdotal things her girls had actually done.

"I think that's a great way to get started. Do Adam and the girls know about it?"

215

"The girls are excited about the idea, especially Martha. Adam mainly warned me about how difficult it is to get published," Anna said with a sigh. "I don't think I can rely on him for a great deal of moral support on this project."

"Just wait 'till you're signing copies at Barnes and Noble! Then he'll eat his words," Charlotte said hotly.

Anna smiled gratefully at her friend. That was the kind of passionate support she needed at this stage, not dire warnings for her own good.

"And what about you, Barbara?" Charlotte asked, turning her attention, "You look like the cat that ate the canary."

"I'm really excited, actually. I got to talking with George about how I'd love to turn my cooking to a profit somehow, and he had the best idea!" She sat beaming at her friends.

"Well, what is it, already?" Charlotte demanded.

"Box lunches!"

"What?"

"George said that at his office they're often calling restaurants for lunch deliveries, you know, when

216

they have meetings through lunch time. Lots of businesses do that sort of thing. Well, he suggested I start my own business advertising home-made box lunches that I would deliver to offices. I could have different menus printed so they could choose, say, box lunch A, B or C."

"That way you could limit the things you offer and the ingredients you'd need," Anna said.

"And you could offer a vegetarian option, or a low-carb option!" Charlotte added.

"Exactly! Wouldn't that be fun? Of course, I have to go through all the steps of getting a small business license and a license to sell food, and all of that. But, it would be worth it to have my very own little business!"

"And you could add yummy extras, you know, like a breath mint or piece of gum."

"And you could charge extra for a small dessert!"

"That's really exciting, Barbara!" Anna said.

"I know! I can't wait to get started. This would be a perfect thing to do during the school day when the house is empty, and I'll finally be making money of my own."

Anna found herself envying her friends a bit. Both of their goals seemed so much more immediately do-able than hers. Was she reaching too far? But, then, wasn't that the point of this whole thing? It would be easier and more clear cut for Anna to choose to begin her own home decorating business or something, but that wasn't her dream. Was it more important for her to just accomplish 'something' or to accomplish 'the' thing? She decided she'd hold out for 'the' thing as long as possible.

..... Several days later Anna awoke with the tell-tale signs of the onset of a cold. Her throat was scratchy and irritated, and even hot tea yielded no relief. She pushed through her day, trying to ignore the symptoms, but by that evening she finally admitted defeat. Her head felt stuffed with cotton, her left eye continually watered, and she had a low grade fever of 99.5. Of course, Adam had a late dinner meeting that night, so Anna still had to get the girls fed, bathed and in bed by herself. She shuffled around in her bathrobe, suffering feverish chills and cursing Adam's name. There's nothing like illness to bring about irrational hate thoughts aimed at the healthy. By the time she fell on her face in bed that night, she'd halfway convinced herself that Adam had intentionally planned his meeting in order to avoid helping her.

Anna prided herself on staying generally healthy, even through the worst of cold season. That made it all the ruder when four days later she was still not much better. She wasn't getting worse; her symptoms were just slightly different each day. Inevitably she reached the stage of having one or both nostrils clogged. There is nothing, absolutely nothing worse than struggling to breathe through your nose. Your whole focus and purpose in life is to get air to pass through your nostrils. Then comes that glorious moment when you do finally feel a clearing and can breathe. It feels as awe-inspiring as a sunrise. Or, equally momentous for Anna was when one of her ears popped and she no longer felt she was speaking and listening from the bottom of a well. The problem was that the next time she blew her nose or sneezed, her nostrils would clog again and her ears would fill.

It was 4 a.m. and Anna was sitting up on the couch, wide awake, struggling to breathe and watching re-runs of Three's Company when the phone rang.

"Heddo?" Anna asked hesitantly.

219

"Anna?"

"Yes, id me. I hab a cold."

"Oh, it's Matt, we're here at the hospital, Faith went into labor around two this morning, and I just wanted to let you know she's fine so far, they're guessing she'll deliver closer to lunchtime." He managed to get all that out in one breath.

"Are you doing okay?" Anna asked.

"Yeah, yeah, I'm fine, I'll keep you updated, alright, I'd better go now, bye." Click.

Anna smiled and hung up the phone. Poor Matt. She remembered what a basket case Adam had been as a first time dad years ago.

Faith was having her baby!

Anna had to fight the urge to wake the household. Everyone would be getting up in a couple of hours, anyway. Then she frowned. With her cold, she probably shouldn't go near the baby, or Faith, for that matter. Darn it all! She'd wanted to help out, especially once Faith was home. Anna picked up the phone again and dialed her mom's number.

"Hello?"

"Hi, Mom, it's Adda."

220

"Anna? Are you okay?"

"I hab a cold. Did Matt call you?"

"Yes! Isn't it exciting?"

"Are you going to de hospital?"

"Well, since she only wanted Matt in the delivery room, I think I'll just wait 'till he calls to say she's had the baby."

"I was godda see de baby, too, but I guess I'll hab to wait 'till my cold's gone."

"Yeah, I guess that would be the safest thing. I'm sorry. Just take care of yourself and then you can help her after she's home. Faith'll understand. That's when she's really gonna need your support, anyway."

"I know. I'm just disappointed."

"I know, sweetie. I'm sorry. Try to get some rest. We'll keep in touch today, okay?"

"Okay, bye, Mom."

"Bye."

Anna put down the phone. If only she could rest! Max jumped onto the couch and snuggled beside her. She held his head and looked into his deep brown hound dog eyes.

"I lub you." He looked at her adoringly. The rest of the family had avoided Anna like the plague the past few days. It was comforting to have at least one loyal buddy. The cats, fickle by nature, tended to desert her during her coughing fits--either because her body was shaking violently or because she looked completely undignified. Even Max, actually, disapproved of her cough drop breath. He usually licked her face almost compulsively, but these days his greetings had become distanced. It made Anna think of Hollywood women 'kissing' the air on either side of one another's cheeks.

"Oh well, I dow you lub me," Anna said to Max.

Stroking his silky beagle-like ears, she returned to absently flipping channels. She hadn't felt much like reading, and even though she knew she should be using all this wakeful time to write, her heart wasn't in it. She'd written a first draft of the 'haircut' story before she got sick, but had progressed no further. Besides these sleepless moments at night, Anna really hadn't had any 'time off' during her illness. That was one of the drawbacks of being Mommy. You never got a sick day. If Adam had felt this crummy, he would have called in sick and spent the day in bed being waited on. Anna,

222

though, had still had to get the girls ready for school, drive them to school, walk Max, pack lunches and make dinners. Her 'free time' had been spent trying to breathe.

Flipping from one paid programming to another, Anna knew that this was the absolute worst time to analyze her life, but she couldn't seem to help it. There's nothing like being sick to set the mood for feeling sorry for oneself. She truly believed if she practiced enough, she could 'think' herself back into wellness. But, at that moment she really didn't feel like trying. Instead, she allowed her thoughts to move from one misery to another. Faith was going to have a new, beautiful baby and her life would be wonderfully transformed. Barbara was on the brink of a fulfilling and lucrative business all of her own making; Adam instantly gained respect from anyone as soon as they learned he was a doctor. Even Martha and Lucy progressed continually, learning new skills, growing and moving from grade to grade. How was Anna progressing? What did she have that was all hers, that was 'her thing'? Okay, so she'd been working on her thoughts and attitudes, but where had it really gotten her? Where were the concrete results?

Anna could feel the old 'darkness' slipping over her. It frightened her, because she hadn't felt that deep depression for some time now. For many years after having Martha, Anna had suffered from pretty severe depression. She hadn't realized quite how severe it had been until she began climbing her way out and could look back. She used to think of suicide virtually every day. She never actually attempted it, but it was on her mind quite a bit. She was overweight, lonely and disappointed in herself. By dropping out of graduate school, she felt a failure and no longer knew who she was. When her world shifted overnight from building a promising career to changing diapers, she'd lost her identity. None of her friends or family were starting families. The trend had become career first, babies second. At 24 years old, Anna had bucked the trend by becoming a young stay-at-home mother, and she felt terribly isolated. All the other 'homemakers' were ten years her senior and at a far different stage in life.

With Adam in medical school, they were new parents living off of loans. Even when he became a resident, they were barely making it from paycheck to paycheck. So, with little Martha and then baby Lucy to raise, Anna also began babysitting kids in her home to try and make ends meet. They were living hours away from any family, so Anna felt more overwhelmed and isolated than ever. Those had been some very dark years for her. She used to gaze at the old black-and-white movies and envy the actors, not because their lives were simpler or glamorous, but because their lives were over. At barely 30 years old Anna often found herself wishing she had more years behind her than stretching out before her. It had only been within the last couple of years that she began climbing up out of her pit of depression, trying to want to live again.

That was why the idea of thoughts having power to create and the law of attraction were so vital to Anna. It gave her hope and power. Her life didn't have to stay the way it was, and she didn't have to wait for circumstances to change gradually on their own. Anna snuggled closer to Max and kissed his little warm head. Beginning to finally feel drowsy, she curled up on her side and pulled a blanket up to her chin. She felt her eyelids droop as she starred unfocused at the flickering television screen. It annoyed and sometimes worried her that she still had these dark, bleak feelings of fear--fear

225

that she was wasting her life; fear that life would remain years of struggle. And now, she feared she wasn't using these new ideas correctly. Maybe it wasn't enough to generally understand or even believe in the law of attraction and power of thoughts. What if it took years and years of practice? What if she never quite mastered it and never got any real, lasting results? What, if like in graduate school, her friends moved on to great accomplishments while she only put in years of effort and got left behind with no results?

Anna drifted into a fitful, troubled sleep and almost immediately entered a powerful dream.

She was swimming in the ocean toward a small island. The choppy water felt icy, and the waves were huge. Anna knew she had to reach the island, but it seemed each swell of the water was carrying her further away. She felt afraid, and her energy was waning. Every other wave was crashing over her head, sending her struggling to fight her way to the surface again for air. After what seemed an eternity, she finally reached the island. Crawling onto shore, gasping for breath, she collapsed in the sand. She lay on her back, staring up into the blue sky and feeling her body warmed by the sun. As her breathing slowed, she felt first great relief, and then a growing peace and sense of accomplishment. 'I made it,' she thought, 'I actually make it.'

Max yelped in his sleep, apparently having a dream of his own. Anna was briefly startled awake. She rolled over on the couch, thinking 'What a strange dream,' before slipping almost instantly into sleep once again.

She was swimming in the ocean towards an island. The water felt cool and refreshing. She was excited about making her way to the island. Each swell and wave seemed to lift and move her closer to shore. She swam with strong, sure strokes, feeling powerful and resilient, with energy to spare. She felt as if she were gliding towards the island, her anticipation mounting as the distance lessened. Never once did she doubt her ability to reach the shore. The moment arrived as she walked onto the sand, looking about her. The sky was blue; the sun glittered on the water and warmed her skin. She sat in the sand, admiring the view and feeling a growing peace and sense of well being. She was proud of having reached the island and thought, 'I made it. I *made* it.'

Anna awoke, hearing Adam's alarm go off upstairs. After a moment the clanging stopped and all was silent once more. Adam almost always reset the alarm for ten or fifteen minutes of more sleep. Anna stretched and blew her nose, piecing together images and feelings of her dreams. At first she was tempted to dismiss them as water dreams triggered by a need to pee. But, she didn't need to use the bathroom, and these dreams weren't like her usual ones. Generally she had bits and pieces of dreams with no real coherence or chronology. But, these had more of a beginning and end, and she could remember most every part of them.

Anna got up, slipped on her robe and padded into the kitchen to put on the kettle. She wondered how Faith was doing, but figured she'd just have to wait for a call. Matt wouldn't have his cell phone on in the hospital. She couldn't wait to tell Adam and the girls that the baby was finally on its way!

Once she had her steaming cup of tea with honey, she settled back on the couch next to Max. She put the TV channel on the news with the sound down low. Once again the alarm went off upstairs. This time Anna heard her husband up and about, opening drawers and

228

then turning on the shower. She considered just sitting in the bathroom with him, letting the steam open her sinuses. Climbing the stairs seemed like an awful lot of effort, though, so she stayed where she was. Besides, she couldn't shake thoughts of her dreams. She wasn't usually big on interpreting dreams, but somehow this time she felt her dreams carried a message, a lesson of some sort. They had been so real! 'Okay,' she thought, 'what was it all about?' In both dreams she'd been trying to reach a goal, the island. In both dreams she reached her goal, and once there, she'd felt peaceful and pleased with herself. The differences had been her swim there.

In one dream she'd struggled the whole way to the island; she'd been afraid and worried she couldn't make it; everything had seemed against her and she was utterly exhausted by the time she got there. In the other dream, her swim had been easy. The same waves that had been her obstacle became her assistance. She'd felt confident and excited about the island even before her accomplishment. Both times she reached the same ending point, whether the journey was a struggle or a pleasure.

'Hmmm...perhaps that's the whole point,' Anna thought. She had many goals: to lose weight, to be an author, and to move to a new house, to name a few. Deep down if she was honest with herself, she believed it was going to be a struggle to accomplish each of them. Was the dream saying the struggle was unnecessary? Sipping her tea, she thought about that for a moment. The dreams weren't just about struggle versus ease, though. Maybe the real lesson had been about the journey. In the second dream she'd enjoyed the swim as much as the destination. She knew in real life she didn't give a flying flip about the journey to her goals--she just wanted it done! In fact, that was often the source of her dissatisfaction--that the journey was taking too long.

"Hey, dear, how are you feeling?" Adam appeared on the stairs in his shirt and tie, freshly showered and shaved and ready for work.

"About de same. Listen, Faith is at de hospital! She started labor at two dis morning!"

"Really? That's great! Are you going to the hospital?"

"No, I don't dink I should."

"Oh, right."

"I'll go in a day or two when she's home and I'm better."

230

"That's a good idea. You can call her later today. Your mom and Matt's mom will be baby hogs, anyway."

"Dat's true."

Anna and Adam continued to chat as he fixed some hot tea to go in a thermos and gathered a granola bar, a packet of oatmeal and a banana to take for breakfast. He almost always ate at his desk, trying to catch up on paperwork before patients arrived. He walked Max and then kissed Anna on top of her head as an antiseptic goodbye. Ironically, Adam was actually quite 'germophobic.' Anna sometimes wondered how he ever got through his work day. Of course, with his patients it was different: he washed his hands a billion times a day and he didn't have to actually live with any of them.

Once Adam had left, Anna mustered up her energy to get a shower in before the girls awoke. She always felt better after a hot shower and some clean clothes.

Thirty minutes later Anna felt almost human. The steamy shower had helped clear her head a lot; she was clean and dressed with some actual make-up on and she'd pumped herself full of daytime cold medicine.

231

While the girls ate toast and watched cartoons, Anna sipped yet another mug of hot tea. She felt she'd soon float away on a tide of chamomile and honey. Still, it helped her throat and calmed her cough, even if only temporarily.

"When will Aunt Faith have her baby?" Martha asked, drinking her chocolate milk. Anna had told the girls the exciting news as soon as they got up.

"I'm not sure. Hopefully by the time you get home from school you'll have a new baby girl or boy cousin!"

"I hope it's a girl," Martha said.

"It'll be a girl if it's born with a dress on," Lucy said matter-of-factly.

Martha snorted in laughter. Anna wondered if it was too early to explain a few things to her youngest.

"Alright, girls, you need to get dressed and brush your teeth."

.... By lunchtime that day Faith had indeed given birth to a healthy baby girl. Anna had gotten the call around 11:30 and had even been able to talk briefly with Faith. Considering the ordeal she'd just been through, Faith sounded pretty good. They named the baby Isabel

232

Nicole. Anna was already thinking of her little 'Izzy,' though she figured Faith and Matt would hate that diminutive. This was one of Lucy's days at home, so she got to hear the news immediately. Of course, her reaction was, "Yay! We can call her 'Belle' like in Beauty and the Beast! Does she have long brown hair?"

Anna had talked briefly to her mother, too, who had raced to the hospital to be one of the first people to see and hold the little newborn. Anna and Faith's mother had always led a detached sort of life; she was a bit of a loner and held an 'I can take it or leave it' attitude about most things--except, that is, her grandchildren. She was absolutely passionate and tireless when it came to being a grandmother. Anna had been frankly shocked after Martha was born at how interested and involved her mother was from day one. And, even as Martha grew, Anna's mother remained as devoted. She would literally get down on the floor and play pretend for hours. She and Martha even began to have their own secret games and such, and Martha would open up to her granny like she would with no other. The same had been true of Lucy. Granny was and is their favorite person on Earth. Anna believed her mother, herself, had been a bit surprised at

233

her passion for her grandchildren. Apparently the same would be true with her feelings for little 'Izzy.'

Anna wished she could join her mother and sister at the hospital, but she knew she was in no state to drive an hour to Richmond and back again. She was reclining on the couch and completely zoning, staring at 'Little Bear' on TV. Earlier, when she was feeling more human, she had pulled out paper, crayons and a couple of boxes of toys Lucy hadn't played with in awhile. She'd turned 'Nick Jr.' on TV and placed a variety of snacks and drinks out on the coffee table. Now, a couple of hours later, she was so grateful for her forethought. The side effects of all the cold medicine she'd taken were hitting at once, mixing with the common cold symptom of feeling that one's head in stuffed with cotton. Anna felt floaty. All she wanted to do was rest her head. 'This must be what it feels like to be on drugs,' she thought, as she stretched out on the couch and lay her head on a pillow. Though, all the drugs she'd ever taken were the over-the-counter variety.

Anna spent the remainder of the afternoon drifting in and out of sleep. She'd already arranged for a neighbor to collect Martha from school, so she wasn't worried about the time. It seemed each moment she awoke a new cartoon was on: Max and Ruby, Franklin, Maisy...She was vaguely aware of Lucy happily playing around her. She was pretty sure she remembered at one point having 'Little People' figures lined up on her legs. Lucy woke her up to ask, "Mommy, can I have a cookie?" She was standing right in Anna's face with a package of Oreos in her hand. Trying to be a responsible parent, even when half conscious, Anna mumbled, "Eat two and save the rest for tomorrow." At some point later Lucy woke up her mother again. Anna squinted at her daughter's chocolate-smeared face. Standing there with two cookies in each hand, Lucy announced, "I'm pretending it's tomorrow, Mommy, okay?" Anna answered, "Sure, whatever."

By four o'clock Martha had been brought home, and Adam had raced out of the office so as to be home by six. He'd called earlier in the day to get the latest baby news and could tell Anna needed to have a night off for rest. As soon as Adam walked through the door, Anna rolled off the couch and stumbled upstairs to fall into bed. As Adam prepared spaghetti and later put the girls in the tub, Anna snored soundly. The accumulation of five sleepless nights had finally taken their toll.

235

Anna woke up to a silent house. She glanced at the clock: 12:00 a.m. Adam was sleeping peacefully beside her. Anna shifted under the covers, noticing her clothes were soaked. She'd sweated through them; apparently her fever had broken. She also noticed she could finally breathe. Anna slipped out of bed and out of her clothes. She quietly pulled on some clean underwear and a gown. Putting on her glasses and a pair of slippers, she padded downstairs. Anna settled herself on the couch with a glass of water and the remote. Max lifted his head long enough to look at her quizzically before letting out a sigh and going back to sleep.

As she absently flipped channels, Anna realized she felt worlds better. That long sleep was just what she'd needed. She was finally returning to good health. 'And just in time!" thought Anna. On Friday there was another Enlightened Ladies meeting, and she wanted to visit Faith and help her with little Izzy over the weekend. 'I wonder how Faith's doing?' she pondered. Anna had been an emotional wreck after Martha was born. She didn't know anything about postpartum depression at the time. All she knew was she was exhausted, leaking milk, completely responsible for a new life and she had no idea how to be a mother. It didn't help any that Martha slept little and cried a lot. It had been a very difficult time--which reminded Anna of the dark feelings that had begun creeping back in during her illness. She repressed a shudder. She did not want to go back down the path!

Anna was tired of flipping channels. She needed to get sleepy again. Maybe she should read awhile. She'd finished her last library book and hadn't felt well enough to get more. So, she got up and went to her desk, where she kept Annie McDowell's essays. She brought the folder back to the couch and tucked herself under a blanket. During her illness she'd felt as if she'd fallen off the planet. Now Anna was eager to get back into life-- continue writing, seeing friends and family and exercising.

The paper she pulled out of the folder was entitled 'Impatience'. Stifling a yawn, Anna began reading:

Impatience

What's really going on when we feel impatient about something? Most of the time when I feel restless or dissatisfied with life it's because I'm impatient for change to happen. I'm waiting and waiting for something, no

237

matter what it is, to happen, to become visible in my life and I'm getting tired of waiting. Eventually I'm not as excited about the thing happening as I am irritated that it isn't here yet.

So, again I ask, what's really going on when I'm feeling impatient? The answer is: I'm not believing. Think about it for a moment. Let's say you have a vacation planned for July. You're going to the beach, and you're so excited. The hotel reservations are made, the dates are marked off and all the arrangements are organized. Between now and July how would you feel? Now and then you may feel a little impatient or frustrated that your vacation isn't here yet. For the most part, though, you'd be happy every time you thought of it and excited that it was coming. You may even do little things to get ready, like shop for a bathing suit or buy new luggage. And you'd do those little preparatory errands with pleasure and anticipation. In other words, you'd enjoy the waiting time as well as the vacation itself. Why? Because you trusted and completely believed that in due time you would have that vacation. There was no fear or doubt in your mind.

You see, I think sometimes we feel that
impatience is almost a good thing. We think it shows us
just how much we want our goal. We think it's our right
and proves the level of our desire. But, desire is supposed
to be a pleasurable experience, not a frustrating one.
There's a big difference between being impatient for
something and anticipating something. One feels bad and
the other feels good. So, when you feel impatient about a
goal, I think it's a red flag indicating that deep down
you're not believing and trusting that your goal is on its
way to you. It's your cue to step back and examine your
true beliefs and expectations. What can you do to
convince yourself that your goal is on its way? Do you
need to alter your beliefs or your goal? You'll know
you're on the right track when your impatience turns to
anticipation!   The most powerful way you can ensure
that a goal is on its way to becoming a reality is to be
truly excited about it long before it ever appears. That's
what 'blind faith' is all about.

Anna put down the paper and took a drink of her
water. 'I never really looked at impatience like that,' she
thought as she hunkered down further beneath the
blanket. It reminded her somewhat of the dream she'd

239

had--that idea of enjoying the journey as much as the destination. Anna rarely enjoyed the journey--metaphorically and literally. Whether it was actually driving in the car or flying on a plane or moving through the steps toward a goal, she always just wanted to get there. She'd figured that being impatient for results was just part of her nature, her personality. She was sometimes almost proud of it, as if her impatience proved her to be a determined, driven person. Instead, perhaps her impatience revealed a deep-set fear that things wouldn't really work out. Not only that, but it robbed her of any opportunity to enjoy the 'scenery' along the way.

Anna turned off the light and stretched out on the couch. Max jumped off his spot on the recliner and joined her, curling into a ball at her legs. Anna yawned and pulled the blanket up to her chin. 'So, what can I do to turn my impatience into anticipation?' She remembered she hadn't done any visualization in quite some time. 'Maybe I should devote more energy to imagining the results I want and to looking at those collages I made.' If the cause of her impatience was a disbelief that the results would ever happen, then she needed to change her belief. She must find a way to believe with all her heart that she

240

was going to lose weight, she was going to be published and she was going to move to a beautiful home. Anna reminded herself that a belief is simply a thought focused on over and over. To form a new belief, she needed to think a new thought, repeatedly. So, as she drifted off to sleep, she thought, 'beautiful body, beautiful home, bountiful success, beautiful body, beautiful home.....'

CHAPTER NINE

"Okay, this is the deal. Everyone take your marker and write your name on your own box of Thin Mints," Anna instructed.

It was March--Girl Scout cookie time. In Anna's household Thin Mints were a hot commodity, so this year they'd ordered five boxes: one for Anna, Adam, Martha, Lucy and one marked 'family' to be used for school lunches. Anna had learned her lesson last year by ordering too few boxes. Things had become nasty and pretty soon accusations were flying as to who had eaten more than their fair share of Thin Mints. This year there could be no arguments.

Anna, Martha and Adam had labeled their boxes. Lucy went to her daddy for help with hers.

"How do you write 'Lucy' again, daddy?" She asked with her marker poised over the box.

"You spell it A-D-A-M," he said slowly.

"Adam!"

"It was worth a try."

It was Martha's second year as a Brownie. This time of year it seemed the family slept and breathed cookies. Anna helped to man all the sales in front of banks and grocery stores; Adam got roped into selling them to everyone at the office, and Lucy was a sort-of Brownie groupie. She tried to linger at their meetings as long as possible and even managed to make her own vest with badges by gluing bits of paper all over her once nice cardigan.

Anna was proud of Martha's dedication, and she certainly supported Girl Scouts herself. But, the entire process was completely foreign to her. With a single working parent, Anna and Faith had never had a chance to join any organizations. So, Anna had felt a bit like a Girl Scout virgin at first (that can't be the best way to word it.) She had no idea about handbooks, pledges, badges, try-its and so on. She and Martha learned together.

Anna felt especially harried this year, however, because she had quite a lot going on besides the cookie sales. Every spare moment she'd been writing. The more she wrote, the more ideas came to her. She'd written and revised almost a dozen little short stories involving her daughters. At the suggestion of the Enlightened Ladies, she'd also been researched different magazines and journals and their submission guidelines. She'd purchased

243

two books as well that explained all the publishing lingo and processes. When she tired of writing, she'd read awhile instead, educating herself on the ins and outs of this bizarre business. So far she'd found three or four magazines she was tailoring some of her stories for, and even a couple of Christian devotional publications looking for inspirational family anecdotes. None of them paid anything, but she had to start somewhere. What surprised her the most was how much she was enjoying all of it, even before she had anything concrete to show for it.

When she wasn't writing or Girl Scout cookie selling, Anna had been visiting Faith and the new baby. On Lucy's at home day, Anna drove Martha to school and then she and Lucy would travel an hour to Faith's and stay there until it was time to collect Martha. While Faith was on maternity leave, Anna wanted to spend time with her and the baby and help out all she could. It also gave Lucy a chance to know her baby cousin and get some experience caring for an infant. It had been funny to see it all through Lucy's eyes. At one point she was holding little Izzy (they all called her that now), and Lucy wrinkled her nose. "Why does she smell cheesy, Mommy?" she asked suspiciously.

Anna laughed, "It's just because she spit up some." Anna became almost wistful at the smell of baby sit-up. It felt like it had been forever since her own children were at that stage. At the time it seemed they'd remain helpless infants indefinitely, but in retrospect that was an all too brief phase. Poor Faith was having difficulty appreciating it at the moment, though. Breastfeeding was a struggle for both her and Izzy; Faith was sleep deprived; she was weeping over the tiniest of issues, and of course, worry over returning to work soon was always weighing on her mind.

"I just don't know how I'm gonna do this," Faith said, fighting back tears. Anna had warned Lucy that all new moms cry some.

"I go back to work in three weeks. How are we gonna pay for childcare? How can I get Izzy ready every day and to the sitter's and get through my work day when I'm up all night?" Before Anna could respond, Lucy sat by her aunt, and patting her arm said, "It's okay, Aunt Faith, all mommies cry." The tender gesture was more than Faith could handle. She dissolved into sobs.

245

Once she'd calmed down, Anna attempted to help her gain some perspective.

"Sweetie, right now is one of those times in your life when you really do have to take it one day at a time. Your hormones are still all over the place. Your body is literally healing from the birth itself; you're not getting enough sleep, and you're feeling the huge responsibility for this new helpless little person."

Faith sniffed. Lucy nodded wisely and stroked her aunt's arm. She was enjoying her role as supporter and confidante.

Anna continued, "When you go through times like this, where it's all you can do to just get through the day, you need to go back to square one."

"What do you mean?"

"Be grateful for what is good in your life, like Matt, your home, the fact that you have a good job waiting for you, the sitter you found who you're pleased with, and of course, little healthy Izzy."

"I feel like I am trying."

"I know, it's hard right now. Sometimes when I'm having trouble feeling good about anything, all I can

246

do is remind myself of what I believe deep down even if I'm not feeling it at the moment."

"Like what?"

"Well, like God has never let you go under financially, even when times were tough. And, God brought you Izzy, so He's going to make it work somehow. Also, any mother can tell you that this is the hardest time. With each week it will get more and more do-able."

"Are you sure?" Faith asked, a little desperately.

"Absolutely."

.... Faith was still on Anna's mind the following week as she drove to the YMCA. How did you keep up with your thoughts and try to attract good things during the roughest times in your life? Anna remembered how she felt the week she was sick and what Faith was going through right now. When you're sick, exhausted, depressed or grieving, is it even realistic to hold a good thought and change your feelings? But, isn't it then that you needed to use those principles the most? Anna parked and entered the gym. She stretched awhile and then climbed on the elliptical machine in a distracted sort of way.

247

How do you attract good thoughts and feelings to you when all you feel is crummy? It doesn't seem realistic to jump from depression to glee. Anna figured in times like those the worst thing to do would be to dwell any longer than necessary on how bad life was. The only thing you could do is reach for a thought or belief that makes you feel a little better or more peaceful.

Anna sighed as she pumped her legs and arms. Some days she felt like she'd never get it all correct. It was a very different way of thinking. She knew she was also struggling with a new phase of this whole experiment. What do you do if you feel you've been working on your thoughts and expectations and then nothing's really changing in your life?

Gazing at her bobbing reflection in the mirror, Anna felt a wave of darkness wash over her. She was getting discouraged, and that scared her a bit. Not because she feared old depression creeping in, but because she realized how truly and completely she'd come to believe these new principles. She needed them to be true, because she simply couldn't return to her old way of thinking and living. That life was full of struggle, chance,

248

helplessness and victimization. She needed power, results, expectation and purpose.

As Anna moved through the weight machines in a robotic way, she pondered why she was feeling down. One biggie was her weight (no pun intended). She'd lost less than ten pounds since Christmas time and now it seemed to have stalled altogether. She'd been trying to take time to visualize herself thin and dwell on those types of thoughts. She was just so used to being this size that it was hard to truly believe she'd ever change, much less see it clearly in her head.

With a sigh, Anna headed to the locker room. Fifteen minutes later she was on her way to meet the other Enlightened Ladies. It was with a certain grim satisfaction that Anna noticed how the steel gray sky matched her desolate mood. She was actually dreading today's meeting, for two reasons: first, her heart just wasn't in it. The last thing she felt like doing was being perky and optimistic. Secondly, she didn't feel like sharing her writing progress. The truth was, she'd gotten a rejection letter the day before. It still stung to think about it. On top of everything, she'd gingerly approached Adam the other day about when they should start thinking

249

about moving. With spring being just around the corner, she'd hoped he'd surprise her by agreeing they should put the townhouse up for sale this summer. Instead, he'd said certainly they should be thinking of selling--in two years or so!

Anna realized she was actually fighting back tears as she searched for a parking space. 'I've got to get myself together,' she thought. It just seemed that the progression of all her main goals--weight loss, being published and moving to her dream home were simultaneously shrieking to a violent halt.

......   "I know I'm being silly. Writers get lots of rejections before they get anywhere, and I'm just a beginner, for goodness sake!" Anna toyed with her coffee stirrer, trying not to let her emotions escape, betraying how truly upset she was. Of course, the worried glance that passed between Charlotte and Barbara revealed they already knew their friend was really struggling.

"I guess I was just so sure that somehow my thoughts would make it happen, with my very first attempt," Anna said with a bitter little laugh that held no amusement. Before her friends could respond, Anna went on to list her other failures in the areas of weight loss and house selling.

"So, I'm no farther along than I was six months ago," Anna summed up with a swallowed sob.

"Now, I do not believe that," Barbara said firmly, "and deep down I don't think you do either."

"I don't know what to believe anymore," Anna said, defeated.

"Believe that all your goals are still on their way. It just may not happen the way you had in mind," Barbara said.

"That's right," Charlotte agreed. "Remember, the how and when of your goals aren't up to you-that's God's job."

"Besides, what's your alternative?" Barbara asked in her ever-so-practical way. "Do you really want to go back to living like you were, like we all were, just getting through each day, some good, some bad, hoping life would treat us well and then sitting back and taking whatever came?"

"Of course not, but this feels almost just as bad-hoping and waiting, with no good results in sight."

"But, just because you don't see the results in their completion doesn't mean they aren't still coming together behind the scenes."

"Exactly," Charlotte agreed, "I think all you need to do, Anna, is stay willing to believe it can still be yours. It's okay if you don't feel it-just be willing to stay open to the possibilities."

Anna sighed. "Well, I think that's all I can do right now. I certainly can't pretend that I feel very positive about anything."

"For now, do like Charlotte says, just say open. Then, when you're ready, I think the next best thing you can do is take action. Keep sending out your stories; keep writing; keep going to the gym; try new, healthier recipes. Even start talking to a realtor yourself."

"What?"

"You don't have to go behind Adam's back. Tell him you're going to start looking online and talking to a realtor. It's never too early to educate yourselves and see what the market's like. See what's out there."

.... "Mommy, Mommy, look! God did a miracle!" Lucy dragged her mother over to the chocolate box Adam had received from one of his patients.

"What?" Anna asked, confused.

"Just look, Mommy!" Lucy dramatically lifted the lid and pointed to the chocolates. Anna smiled. The night before, she and Adam had finished off the top layer and had removed the partition to reveal a second complete layer. Apparently Lucy hadn't realized another layer existed.

"Yes, sweetie, that's amazing!"

"Isn't God wonderful?" Lucy asked.

"Yes, He sure is." Anna chuckled to herself as she returned to her ironing. She wondered how Lucy would handle it when the seemingly endless box of chocolates was truly emptied. Still, it was refreshing to see such ready belief in the possibility of miracles.

She finished one of Adam's shirts and began spraying starch on the next. It had been a couple of weeks since she'd met with her friends, and, thanks to their loving advice, her life felt better. Nothing dramatic had changed, really. It was just that her peace and hope had returned. For a few days she did as Charlotte suggested and simply reminded herself to stay willing to believe and accept good things. After awhile she felt strong enough to follow Barbara's suggestion of taking

253

action. She continued her workouts and recommitted herself to following the Slimfast plan. She'd had to admit to herself that she had let that diet regime slip quite a bit since the holidays. She'd also been e-mailing a realtor to see the direction they may want to take.

Anna finished the last shirt and hung it up carefully. She didn't particularly enjoy ironing, but she had to admit the finished product was rewarding.

"Now, on to the pants," Anna said to herself.

"What, Momma?" Martha asked, wandering into the room munching on an apple.

"Oh, I'm just talking to myself. I'm done with your dad's shirts. Now I have the pants to do."

"It looks like fun. I wish I could help."

"Believe me, so do I!" Anna smiled. She'd tried to show Martha some ironing basics not long ago, but it quickly became clear that she wasn't quite big enough. When Anna told Adam she was trying to see if Martha could take over with ironing, he'd looked horrified. As it turned out, he wasn't so much distressed over Martha's safety as he was concerned about the state his clothes would end up in. "I'll tell you how you could help, Martha."

254

"Sure, what?"

"You could read the latest story I wrote and let me know what you think."

"Yeah, that's no problem. Are you gonna send out more to publishers?"

"Yes, as soon as I've looked them over more." Another action Anna had taken was to revise all her stories once again and add a few more. She'd also pulled out the rejection letter again to see exactly where she should improve.

"But, you know, one of the suggestions from that other publisher was that my stories would sell themselves better if they had illustrations. I'm not sure what to do about that."

"I could draw some pictures," Martha said hopefully.

"Well, maybe, but I'm wondering if they want more professional drawings," Anna said carefully.

Martha grunted a reply as she took a bit of her apple and chewed awhile. "I bet Granddad could draw professionally," she said matter-of-factly.

Anna stopped in her ironing. She'd never thought of her father, but, of course, he'd do a fabulous

255

job. She stared off into space for a moment, considering the possibility.

"Mom, shouldn't you move the iron?"

"Oh, gosh, yes," Anna quickly picked up the iron, relieved it hadn't yet left a scorch mark.

"That's a good idea, Martha! I'll see if my dad would do the illustrations. Of course..." Anna hesitated.

"What is it?"

"Well, I guess I'm just a little nervous about him reading my writing. I hope he likes the stories."

"Of course he will! They're wonderful. Besides, he has to--he's your dad!"

CHAPTER TEN

"Whose idea was this, anyway?" Barbara laughed, half amused and half irritated, as she defended her blueberry muffin from an aggressive goose.

"They'll leave us alone in a minute if we don't feed them anything," Anna said, clutching her bagel close to her chest. She was all too aware it had been her suggestion that they meet at the pond this time. It was a gorgeous day in early April--one of those first spring days that holds a gentle warmth and carries the sweet fragrance of blooming daffodils and tulips. To sit inside a dark restaurant on such a day would be blasphemous.

Sure enough, after a few moments the geese and ducks retreated, and the Enlightened Ladies could enjoy their coffee and baked goods in peace. After swallowing a bite of her bagel, Anna remembered, "Oh, Barbara, Adam said he would talk to the powers that be at his office about them using you for their next dinner meeting. I gave him your menus."

"Thanks! This is so exciting! After all the time getting licenses and planning and advertising, I'm actually getting orders."

257

"How's it been so far?" Charlotte asked.

"Well, I've only done two box lunch orders, but the comments were good. I'm definitely learning as I go, but I guess there's no other way to do it. What about you, Charlotte?"

Charlotte took a sip of coffee before answering. She'd been a regular volunteer at a local animal shelter for weeks. "Actually, I'm pretty excited. You know I decided to work on training some of the dogs, to make them easier to get adopted? Well, I've been talking with Petsmart. They've agreed to use our dogs, one each session, as examples in their obedience classes, and advertise them as available for adoption!"

"Oh, what a great idea!" Anna and Barbara chorused.

"Yeah, this is going to make such a difference. I really think we can place a lot of the dogs this way. As for the cats, I thought I might look into taking them to nursing homes for therapy and company. Again, we could then advertise them for adoption in a broader area."

"I think you're really onto something, Charlotte. You're certainly doing a lot more for the shelter than just cleaning cages and filing papers!"

258

"Thanks," Charlotte said with a broad smile, "I think I'm finding my calling."

There was a comfortable silence as the women gazed at the peaceful scene before them and finished their breakfast. Anna felt maybe her friends were uneasy about asking how she was progressing. It was with pride that she pulled out of her tote bag her collection of short stories, along with her father's illustrations.

"Have a look at these," she said.

Her friends gasped, "Anna, these are beautiful! Did you draw them?"

Anna snorted, "Certainly not! No, my dad did. Aren't they perfect?"

"They completely bring your stories to life!" Charlotte observed.

"And, are these some new ones?" Barbara asked, looking at the last several pages.

"Yeah, I've added a few stories and changed some of the other others, too. I think I'm about ready to send them to publishers."

"I think this could truly lead to something, Anna."

"Really?"

259

"Definitely!"

....   That evening while preparing dinner Anna found
herself thinking about what her friends had said. She was
so pleased at their enthusiasm, but she was scared, too.
She hated to voice her fears aloud, but...what if she
continued to get only rejection letters? How could she
handle it if time after time she raised her hopes for
nothing? She knew she shouldn't dwell on the negative
possibilities, but it was hard not to.

"Okay," Anna said aloud, "I need to focus on
what I want-- to be published and have a successful
writing career. I need to remember that I'm attracting
what I'm always thinking about. So, I need to think about
getting that letter or phone call that says 'we want to
publish your manuscript'!

"Who are you talking to, Mommy?"

Anna jumped. "Oh, Lucy, hi. I was just talking
to myself. Don't you ever do that?"

"No."

"Oh."

"Only if I'm talking to my imaginary brother,
Sam. Who's your imaginary friend, Mommy?"

"Well..." Anna was saved from having to reply by the ringing of the telephone. "Hold on, sweetie." Anna picked up the phone. "Hello?"

"Hi, Anna," answered Faith.

"Hi! I haven't talked to you in awhile. I figured you've been pretty busy now that you're back at work."

"Yeah, I have been. It's been hard. We're already starting to feel the pinch financially of adding formula, diapers and daycare to our budget."

"I can imagine. I wish I knew what to suggest. Is Matt still looking for a better job?"

"Yeah, he's got his resume out everywhere, but so far nothing."

"And how is Izzy?"

"She's fine, but her sleeping schedule is still all over the place!"

"Well, that will come. Before you know it she'll turn a corner and begin a new phase that will give you all a bit more routine."

"I hope you're right! Look, I need to go. Sorry I've called and just dumped on you. Are all of you okay?"

"Yeah, we're fine. Call and dump on me any time! Love ya!"

261

"Love ya, too. Bye!"

Anna sighed as she hung up the phone. She remembered how hard things are with a new baby, especially the first. At least for the majority of her mothering years, she hadn't had to try and juggle an infant and a full time job. All she knew to do was put in prayers for Faith and hold expectations for some helpful changes in their lives.

Anna returned to her dinner preparations just as Lucy came wandering back into the kitchen.

"I forgot to bring anything for show and tell today."

"Oh, I'm sorry, dear."

"So I told my class how my Mommy's a writer."

Anna stopped chopping a carrot in mid-slice. "What?"

"My teacher wants me to bring one of your books in for show and tell tomorrow."

"What?! Oh, honey, I don't really have any books--"

"You have stories and Granddad's pictures."

"Yeah, but--"

"Can I bring one of those tomorrow, Mommy, please? Mrs. Chase wants to see it."

"Well, I guess."

"Yay! Don't forget to put it in my pack-pack!" Lucy called over her shoulder as she skipped out of the room.

Anna put down the knife and plopped into a kitchen chair. She somehow felt weak all of a sudden. She guessed it was just the act of proclaiming herself as a writer to anyone but her close friends. It made the whole business seem real and scary. She felt like she was bluffing, like she was a fraud trying to con others. She took a few deep breaths and tried to get some perspective.

'Okay,' thought Anna, 'this is not that big a deal. I'll send a story or two with Lucy and write a note to Mrs. Chase explaining that I'm not yet a published author. It's just a few preschoolers listening to the stories, anyway. They'll hardly be ruthless critics.'

Feeling somewhat calmed, Anna finished pulling together dinner, but she never could quite stop mulling over this new development.

...... A week later, however, Anna was feeling let down and trying to deny it to herself. Nothing much had

263

really come of the grand debut of Anna's stories. Anna had carefully chosen two that she thought the preschoolers may appreciate. Most of them were geared toward older elementary school ages. Lucy said her classmates liked them, though, and Mrs. Chase was very sweet and supportive. That had pretty much been it. Anna had envisioned much greater results. Her hopes had quickly soared that this show and tell moment would be her big break. Somehow one of the parents would be helping out in the classroom who just happened to be taking the day off from his or her publishing job. Upon hearing Anna's stories the parent would track her down and insist on signing her to a contract...or something along those lines.

When life just continued as normal, Anna found it difficult to recapture her excitement for writing. She wasn't exactly depressed, she just felt a bit deflated. She didn't really want to admit how she was feeling to anyone, including herself. She felt foolish for having raised her hopes over such a minor incident in the first place. Did she really expect a preschool show and tell to make her famous?!

264

So, Anna pressed on with forced cheerfulness. She continued her mantra of positive declarations: I'm becoming thin; I'm moving toward having my dream home...However, one wet Wednesday in April Anna finally snapped. She had just put a sheet of baking cookies in the oven. She knew she shouldn't be eating them, but there was just enough in the cookie dough roll for four cookies, and she didn't think anyone would miss them. Besides, the girls were at school, so Anna could claim all the cookies for herself and actually enjoy them in peace. She'd been doing well with her diet, but for some reason these cookies with the extra large chocolate chunks were calling to her today.

"Yow!" Fritz, their Siamese-mix cat was standing at the stairs yelling. He wanted to go out the back sliding door.

"Oh, okay," Anna muttered, following him down the steps to the walkout patio. She was getting completely fed up with letting Fritz and Bess, their tabby cat, in and out of the back door. It was yet another item on her growing mental list of reasons she wanted to move. Adam never had to deal with it, being at work all day. But, for Anna, once spring and summer arrived, she

265

traveled up and down the stairs a dozen times a day letting the blasted cats in and out. With the glass door, they couldn't install a cat door without actually going through the wall. She tried keeping the cats in all the time, but they began rebelling by messing all over the house. Anna dreamed of a home with a convenient cat door through the garage or utility room that would give freedom to both her and the cats.

"Alright, go on," Anna said, sliding open the door. But Fritz just stood there, peering at the rainy patio with disdain. How dare it be wet when His Highness wished to go for a stroll?

"Just go on, Fritz!" Anna knew if she tried to push or throw him out, he'd just run back into the house and keep bugging her. His slanted green eyes stared at her accusingly. It was obviously her fault that the weather wasn't cooperating. Before Anna could defend herself, Max came tearing down the stairs. The rain had kept him cooped up, too, and he was full of restless energy.

"Max, no!" But, it was too late. Fritz dashed outside, with Max right on his heels. Anna had to run out in the rain, tackle Max, drag him inside and try to

266

thoroughly wipe them both down before they tracked mud all over the carpet. Anna finally climbed the stairs only to be met with the undeniable smell of burning cookies. She ran to the stove and pulled out the sheet of four little black bricks. Anna slumped into a kitchen chair and sobbed.

After a few minutes, Anna had cried herself dry. She threw away the cookies and carried a glass of water and a Slimfast bar over to the couch. Instead of turning on the TV, she switched on the stereo to some soothing piano music and sat down to simply think a moment. What in the world was going on with her? She'd thought she was doing okay. 'Or, maybe it's more like I've been working awfully hard to convince myself I'm doing okay.' She reached behind her and grabbed the folder of her grandmother's essays from the desk. Flipping through the pages, her eyes settled on one entitled *'Acceptance'*

Knowing how my thoughts and expectations attract more of the same, what do I do when I can't seem to stop feeling bad about something? Is it best to just deny how I feel? Will that turn things around for me? Or, should I acknowledge how I'm really feeling? But, if I talk about how bad or angry I feel and give in to my emotions, isn't that just keeping me right where I am?

267

I know, you're thinking 'Enough questions, already!' I don't claim to have all the answers, but after much trial and error I've decided one thing: You need to acknowledge how you're feeling before you can change it. Simply admitting how you feel, venting to a friend or having a good cry in private, it's not only okay, it's crucial. I used to think the best course of action was to try and stay positive about any issue from the beginning, no matter what. What I found, though, was the more I tried to convince myself I felt fine about something, the more aware I was of how 'not fine' I was about it. You're always searching for a better feeling, right? Well, I finally came to realize that sometimes simply yelling or crying about a problem did make me feel better--often much better than when I was being falsely cheerful.

So, go ahead, admit it--you're angry, sad, resentful, bitter, whatever. It's okay. It doesn't mean to embrace it and wallow in your misery indefinitely. Just know that you won't feel that way forever, and acknowledging where you're starting from is the only way to get somewhere else.

Anna sighed and took a bite of her Slimfast bar. She knew her breakdown wasn't entirely about the ruined

268

cookies. In fact, it had very little to do with anything that had happened in the past hour. She knew it was the result of keeping her disappointment and frustration bottled up. Even though life had been a bit better lately, she was still impatient for real, concrete results--ones that she could point to and proclaim to the world--'Here, look at this! I did this. Isn't it wonderful?!'

Since no one else was in the house, Anna stated aloud, "Okay, so, yes, I'm disappointed. I'm angry and fed up with God and the Universe, because I feel like I'm doing my part. I've been doing my part for months now! It's time for some supernatural powers to step in and finish the job. Bring me some real results, already! I refuse to settle for a mediocre life. I want a great one! And I know that You want just as much and more for me, so let's get on with it!"

After a couple more minutes of yelling at the Universe, Anna finally felt spent. She knew the timing was supposed to be up to God. In an ideal world, she should be content to be patient. Was her growing impatience an indication that deep down she doubted her goals would ever come true? Of course it was! But, could anyone really erase all doubt from their minds?

269

Anna figured she needed to work a bit more on making her 'belief' quotient outweigh her doubtful one. She knew she'd completely let slip her time of visualizing, meditating and praying. As she began gathering her purse and keys to collect Lucy from school, she tried to end her tumultuous morning on a positive note by mentally listing her blessings again: healthy children, spring days, good friends....

.... "No, Momma, I don't need it! I'm not a baby, is I'm?" Lucy frowned, with little hands on tiny hips.

"Are you sure you don't want your stroller? What if your legs get tired of walking?" Adam asked.

"Then I'll skip!" Lucy answered confidently.

"Oh, come on, everybody." Anna herded the family toward the park entrance. It was an unseasonably warm day in May, already almost eighty degrees at ten a.m. The family had decided to trade their tiny townhouse for the great outdoors by spending all day at Maymont Park in Richmond. The park was one of Anna's most treasured and sacred escapes. She and Faith had been frequenting the park since they were toddlers. Anna and Adam had their second date at Maymont when they were only teenagers. It had been a plantation in the

270

1800's owned by the Dooley family. It had been bequeathed to the city as a public park. Maymont boasted acres of farmland, Italian gardens, Japanese gardens, a nature center and the Dooley mansion itself.

"Momma, can we feed the animals?" Martha asked shyly, yet eagerly. She was always so hesitant to request anything, especially when it involved money. Lucy, on the other hand, already had her little hand thrust out, ready for coins. The park provided 'grain vending machines' as Adam called them.

"Sure, sweetie," Anna replied, struggling to extract two quarters from her coin purse buried deep in the backpack she sported. They had made this day trip so frequently that Anna had it down to a science. They always carried a backpack with coins, cash, wipes, hand sanitizer, sunscreen, food and drinks and Band-Aids. They also carried a rolled up blanket for picnicking, and often bubbles and a ball or Frisbee. She also brought spare clothes and shoes in the car, because someone always fell in one of the many small streams they passed. Of course, Anna realized with a pang, this was the first time without a stroller, sippy cup and diaper bag.

271

'If I hadn't miscarried....no,' she thought firmly, 'I'm not going down any road of self pity or regret. Today is about enjoying and appreciating.'

Anna felt the warming sunshine on her face as she watched her girls gingerly offering grain to the goats and sheep behind the fences. She gave herself a mental pat on the back. She'd been fairly consistent the past few weeks with remembering gratitude and finding the positive in most things. Nothing had advanced much with her writing or her wish to move, but she had lost eight pounds, and that felt good. This was the first time this season she'd worn shorts and a sleeveless top. With her lightly tanned body (from a bottle), French braided hair and newly painted toenails in strappy sandals, Anna felt almost attractive.

"Come on, girls, let's move along," directed Adam.

"Oh yeah, I almost forgot--we're supposed to meet Faith and Matt at the Dooley mansion around noon," Anna added.

The little troop happily wound their way down the hill, past the birds of prey and the bears, on to the Japanese gardens. Anna loved this section of the park, with the waterfall, gazebo, Japanese maples and pond full of enormous koi. Having time to spare, Adam and Anna settled on a bench beside the pond while the girls carefully picked their way across the stepping stones that spanned the shallow water. Anna could hardly look. She sent up a silent prayer, as she did every time, that neither girl would fall in. As Adam watched, cringing and flinching beside her, she figured he was doing the same thing. Perhaps to get his mind off the potential splash, Adam asked, "So, how's the writing going?" Anna tore her eyes from the girls to gaze at him in surprise. He hadn't exactly been supportive, not in any serious way. Anna had deliberately avoided telling him of her numerous rejection letters. She simply couldn't take his unspoken 'Well, I tried to warn you' attitude.

"Um, well, it's okay," Anna answered. "I haven't yet had any offer, though." She knew she was seriously understating the situation.

"Well, you're having fun, though, aren't you?"

Anna hesitated. She suddenly realized that, no, she wasn't having fun anymore. She briefly got a flash of how fun and yummy the writing had first been, before she got burdened with getting results.

273

"Anna?"

"Yeah, sorry. I was just thinking. No, I haven't been enjoying writing lately. I think I've gotten too wrapped up in getting published. It's kind-of colored everything, you know?"

"Well, maybe you need to just write for awhile," Adam suggested.

"Yeah, I think so," Anna agreed. She realized that idea filled her with relief. No one would think any less of her for doing something just for pleasure, certainly not Charlotte or Barbara. She had been the one judging herself and needing tangible results and success.

"Mommy, I'm thirsty," a flushed Martha announced, suddenly appearing at Anna's elbow.

"And I'm starving!" said Lucy.

"Okay, girls, let's head up to the Italian gardens and find Aunt Faith."

Twenty minutes later the entire crew was lounging on picnic blankets, dividing up food, all except Matt.

"I thought Matt was coming, too," Anna said, cuddling Izzy. While Anna inhaled the sweet smell of the baby's head and admired her tiny pea pod toes, Izzy was busy grasping for Anna's sparkly necklace and earrings.

"Matt's at an interview!" Faith announced, bursting with excitement.

"Really?"

"This is his second interview with this company, so it's looking promising. And the job is just perfect. It's working with computers, with a pay increase and really good benefits!" Faith summed up enthusiastically.

"Oh, Faith, how wonderful!" Anna exclaimed while trying to disentangle Izzy's little fingers from her necklace.

"And," continued Faith, "this week I'm changing up my schedule. My manager noticed how run down I was looking, so she suggested I try working three long days and staying home for two. If I worked three ten-hour days, I'd still qualify for benefits and we could pay less for daycare."

"What a good idea!" Anna commented. "Do you think it would work?"

"Well, I'm going to try it this week. It would be worth three marathon work days if I could stay home in my pajamas two days with Izzy."

275

"Can I stay home in my pajamas?" joked Adam.

"I wanna stay home in my jammies two days, too!" insisted Lucy.

"You already do," Martha pointed out enviously.

.... That night Anna prepared a very simple, light dinner. Everyone was tired, grimy and slightly sunburned. No one wanted a heavy meal, and Anna certainly didn't have the motivation to cook it. Instead, she opted for baked chicken breasts with lemon pepper seasoning and a spring salad. Once the weather turned warm, Anna swapped her winter stews for salads, fruits and meat such as fish and chicken. She also eagerly sought out the first hyacinths and daffodils in the grocery stores to bring home and place on the table, filling the house with their perfume. She fully embraced spring as a time of new beginning and rebirth. There was something uplifting about watching the earth come to life again, like a renewed promise each year. She especially cherished April and May, before the crushing heat and humidity of Virginia summers set in.

Finally, by eight o'clock or so everyone had bathed and eaten, and Anna had cleaned up the kitchen and set the coffee timer for Sunday morning. With the

276

girls sleepily watching a movie, Anna could slip away to her room for some quiet time. She was excited to begin writing again, for fun, but felt she was too weary to do it any justice tonight. Instead, she turned on her favorite piano music softly and pulled out her grandmother's writings. She chose an essay entitled '*Just Being Happy.*' The date on this one caught her eye, because it was the last year Annie McDowell had lived. Anna read on...

After decades of living, I've realized the very simplest of truths: I just want to be happy. I want to be happy, that's it--no conditions at all. I want to be happy now, not tomorrow or next month or even later today. See, most of my life I've put off my own happiness: I'll be happy when I have this money or own that or look like this...I've had all these conditions to meet. Even if I was excited about reaching the conditions, they were still holding me back. I'll be happy this June on our trip, or this weekend when we can sleep in...I finally realized I want to be free and unencumbered to be happy now, no matter what. What a relief! What a feeling of liberation to surrender all those conditions. It was a decision I had to make, and to remind myself of repeatedly. Right now I'm simply going to be happy, no matter what money we

277

*have, no matter what I weigh, no matter what day of the
week it is, no matter if the house is a mess, no matter
what! To maintain my resolve, I found I had to do two
things: factor out everyone and everything else and tune
my focus to the things around me that I found pleasing.
Almost any time I began feeling upset, angry or anxious I
realized I was either letting someone or something else
get to me, or I was focusing on something not pleasing. It
took deliberate practice, but what a relief to just be happy
now.*

      Anna slowly put down the paper and sat thinking
over the implications of the idea of being happy now.
Was it too simplistic? Was it somehow irresponsible?
But it was a relief, the thought of letting go of all the
conditions of happiness. There would always be
something more, anyway. Once they moved to their
dream home, they'd want to decorate it. Once she lost the
weight, she'd need to maintain it and get really fit. Once
she was published, she'd be working on more books. You
never finished it all. Anna still wanted to have goals, but
she didn't want to postpone her happiness based on
accomplishing them all. She also didn't want to wait until
the end of her days, as her grandmother had, to have this

278

epiphany. If she granted herself permission to let everything go, think how many more happy days she'd enjoy for years to come. Maybe she should bring this up at the next meeting.

.... "I know it sounds a bit silly, but what if we all try just being happy, no matter what?" Anna suggested. She had just finished explaining her grandmother's advice to Barbara and Charlotte. For a change, the three were seated at a table at in the mall. It was a gray, rainy morning, and Anna wanted to do a little shopping before picking up Lucy.

"I'm all for being happy, but how do you just decide to be happy?" asked Charlotte.

"And how do you quantify something like that?" Barbara asked.

"Well, you can't exactly measure it," considered Anna, "but you can tell when you feel better, kind-of lighter, you know? My grandmother said she had to learn to factor out everyone but herself and to focus only on what pleased her."

"Now, factoring out everyone else would sure make a huge difference. I feel like Chris came downstairs one morning after turning twelve in a bad mood, and it

279

hasn't left yet," Barbara commented. "But wouldn't I be a bad mother if I didn't care?"

"Yeah," agreed Charlotte, "how do I ignore Emma drawing on the walls and having temper tantrums in the middle of the Wal-Mart checkout lane?"

"I know what you mean. Life happens, and you'd have to be a bit insane to be deliriously happy through all of it. I think the idea is to let the annoying parts be a bit more blurry and magnify the good parts. Let Chris be in a bad mood, since nothing you could say could fix it anyway. You being peaceful and happy would probably be the best help to him."

Barbara and Charlotte looked at Anna skeptically.

"I don't know," Anna concluded with a sigh, "I just liked the idea of simply being happy."

"Well, I'd say it's worth a try, anyway," Charlotte agreed, hating to see her friend looking so wilted.

Barbara reconsidered, "You know, all of our nitpicking is actually making your point. It's like we're arguing that we can't be happy. You'd almost think we don't want to be! Ridiculous, isn't it?"

"You're right," laughed Charlotte, "it's deceptively simple. Let's be happy this week!" She put her hand in the middle of the table, with Barbara's on top of hers and Anna's on last, ending in a 'let's go team' type of motion.

CHAPTER ELEVEN

Anna was enjoying one of her guilty pleasures while folding laundry--watching 'The Price is Right.' She was embarrassed to admit it to anyone else, but she found the show somehow comforting. It was bright, happy and simplistic. Amidst all the victories and losses, it remained forever hopeful. Anna had managed to forge a similar strength over the past month or so. She'd become quite adept at focusing on pleasant things and blurring the rest. Even as she tried to fold Lucy's tiny tutu like skirt, Anna was only dimly aware of rather unsavory characters loitering on the sidewalk in front of the townhouses and the thumping beat of car stereos in the parking lot. It was now July, and with the summer heat had begun the twenty-four hour block party. Anna could no longer kid herself that the neighborhood would ever improve. And, her chats with the realtor hadn't been promising, either. The housing market had plummeted just after Anna and Adam bought their townhouse. Their same property would now appraise for less than half of what they bought it for. Their only hope would be to move and rent it out, but with their high mortgage a rent check wouldn't even cut their losses.

Anna began carrying everyone's folded clothes to their dressers just as the next contestant was invited to 'come on down.' She smiled gently as she pondered the change in herself. She felt peaceful. Despite the neighborhood, the summer's relentless heat and the girls being underfoot every day, Anna had reached a liberating point of not caring. Her attitude regarding anything tedious, aggravating or anxiety-producing had become 'this too shall pass.' She had given up--surrendered--waved the white flag--put down her weapons. She'd stopped struggling and fighting--with herself, and it had been such a relief! And her greatest pleasant surprise was that by surrendering, she had actually won. She'd won acceptance, contentment, bits of joy and perhaps most important, a fairly unshakeable feeling of security. She had a deep knowing that everything was fine and everything would be fine.

As Anna placed her shorts and tank tops in their drawers she smiled again. She'd also begun to win in tangible ways, too. Somewhat effortlessly in the past couple of months she'd dropped to a consistent size twelve, with some tens sneaking in. She'd also found new energy and inspiration regarding her writing. By completely letting go of the need to be successful, she'd found such satisfaction in editing her old stories and beginning new ones. Anna and her dad had also forged a new relationship as co-creators. They found that they thought the same way and had a similar sense of humor. Whether or not she was ever published, Anna now had a whole menagerie of short stories, picture books and even a small chapter book she'd written full of her father's illustrations that she could cherish.

Just as Anna put the last shirt in the last drawer the phone rang.

"Hello?"

"I have the most exciting news!" announced Faith.

Anna chuckled. "You're not pregnant again so soon!"

"No, thank goodness," laughed Faith, "Matt has finally and officially got that computer job!"

"Oh, Faith, that's wonderful!"

"But listen to the best part--he's able to do work from home. So, he's going to stay home three days a week while I stay home the other two days. We won't have to do daycare anymore!"

"That's amazing. It's perfect."

"I know, I can hardly believe it," agreed Faith. "It sounds awfully quiet there. Have you shut the girls in the closet or something?"

"No," laughed Anna, "but I've been tempted at times this summer. Actually, they've gone with friends to the public pool. I think they'll be back before long, though."

"In that case, I'll leave you to your moment of peace. I'll call you later. Bye!"

"Bye, and tell Matt 'way to go!'"

Just as Anna was hanging up the phone it rang again. Without waiting for the caller id to operate, Anna answered, "Hello?"

"May I speak with Mrs. Kin?"

'Oh drat,' thought Anna, 'it's a sales call.' She almost fibbed and pretended to be someone else. At the last second she conceded, "This is she."

"Hi, Mrs. Kin. You don't know me. My name is Liz Parker, and I attend the church where your daughter's preschool is."

285

"Oh, yes..."

"Our Sunday school class meets in the same room where the preschool is held. It's a long story, but as I was setting up a little coffee and doughnut area I came across a copy of your children's stories."

"Oh, really?"

"Yes, and well, I know I shouldn't have, but I showed them to my husband. He works in a small firm in D.C. Anyway, he'd like to meet with you if you're at all interested in having your work published."

Anna was in pure shock. She felt weak. Somehow she squeaked out, "Yes, I'd be very interested."

"Oh, good. Again, I apologize for reading your stories, but the drawings caught my eye, and...anyway, my husband's name is Frank. I'll have him give you a call."

"That would be great, thank you." Anna ended the call in a daze. She sank into a chair. Was this for real? Was this how it all worked--as soon as she no longer needed success, it came to find her. Slowly an enormous grin spread across Anna's face.

A sunburned Martha and Lucy stumbled into the house moments later, astonished to find their mother dancing around the living room.

.... "Look, Mommy, I'm swimming!" Lucy proudly declared, little limbs erratically splashing about.

"Good, dear," praised Anna. In reality, Lucy had so many flotation devices strapped on her, she could be perfectly still and remain buoyant.

Not to be outdone, Charlie shouted, "Look, Mom, I gonna dive!" and then proceeded to do a mini cannonball off the diving board.

"Great!" said Charlotte. The afternoon had been one long chorus of 'Look, Mom,' as Charlotte, Anna and Barbara's kids all vied for attention. The Enlightened Ladies had gathered at Barbara's backyard pool. Their summer meetings had been held at parks and pools where all the kids could play while the women chatted.

"So, have you signed a contract yet?" Barbara asked Anna before sipping her lemonade.

"No, I'm having Adam's lawyer look over all the paperwork first. I mean, I have no idea what I'm doing when it comes to the legal side of this." Anna took a bite of watermelon and tried to spit out a seed on her paper

287

plate in a lady-like way. "Anyway, it's only a tiny publishing firm who puts their stuff out to local privately owned bookstores. It's not as if my books will be in the new release section of Barnes and Noble."

"Now, don't you dare down-play this, Anna, " scolded Charlotte. "This is huge, and I have a feeling it's just the beginning for you."

Anna smiled weakly. She'd been trying to tell herself the same thing. It was just, well, it had been one thing to dream of success; it was a very different thing to be actually wading through the nitty-gritty of it all. She'd been having a hard time keeping the good feelings going. Was she doing all of this correctly? Would her books even sell? Would this be the beginning of her writing career or would this be only as far as she ever got?

In between lotioning Emma's little back and shouting "That's great" to Charlie, Charlotte had been studying Anna's face. "You don't look like a woman who's about to take the publishing world by storm. What's the matter?"

Anna sighed and proceeded to outline her fears and how she'd been weighted down by so many details all the sudden.

288

"You know what this reminds me of?" asked Barbara. "It makes me think of buying a house and moving. You know, you start with the grand idea of 'I want to live in that beautiful home.' Then comes finding a good realtor, having appraisals, contracts, negotiations, home inspections, termite inspections and closing. By the time you've packed, arranged for movers and set up all the utilities, you're sorry you ever dreamed of moving at all."

Charlotte and Anna laughed appreciatively. That sure was the truth!

"But," Barbara continued, "two or three weeks later when you're settled in and the essentials are unpacked, you know it was all worth it, because you're there and it's yours."

"Yeah, I guess you're right," conceded Anna.

"Yeah, Anna, it'll all be worth it when your book is actually on the shelves. When will that be, by the way?" Charlotte inquired.

"Not 'till the fall."

"Well, all you can do, I guess, is enjoy the process. Or, at least be glad it's proceeding!"

Before Anna could reply, the three women were startled by an ominous ripping sound. They jumped to
289

their feet (or, more accurately, awkwardly climbed out of their lounge chairs) in time to see Lucy sink to her waist in the middle of the large outdoor trampoline. Apparently all the kids had decided to test out the aging trampoline at one time, and it had torn under the strain. Lucy, of course, had managed to get herself wedged in the tear. Martha was laughing while trying to pull a shrieking Lucy out of the hole.

"Hold on, kids, we're coming!"

CHAPTER TWELVE

"Okay, Martha, you need two packs of No. 2 pencils, and Lucy needs crayons."

"Here, Mommy," said Lucy, struggling to hoist a box of 64 crayons with built-in sharpener into the shopping cart.

"Wait!" protested Anna, "The list says a box of 16, Lucy."

"But, Mommy--"

"Here are the pencils. Now what?" asked Martha.

"Um, let's see, two packs of wide ruled paper."

"And my list says I need this," announced Lucy, throwing a pink Hello Kitty backpack into the cart.

"Lucy, stop," scolded Anna, retrieving the backpack. "You already have a backpack."

"Well, I gonna need all new school clothes and very sparkly shoes."

"Lucy, today we're just getting school supplies. Besides, you'll just keep wearing your summer clothes. You won't need any new fall clothes for months yet."

It was mid-August, and Anna and the girls were among throngs of others finally getting around to school supply shopping. Their county schools began before Labor Day, in the third week or so of August. The date always snuck up on Anna. It was somehow hard to believe it was school time again while it was still scorching hot and pools were open.

Lucy was entering her pre-kindergarten year, so Anna and Adam had decided to enroll her for three full days at her preschool. She could begin adjusting to the 9 a.m. to 3 p.m. school day, but still play at home a couple of days. Lucy saw school supply shopping as a time to capitalize on accessories: shoes, lunch boxes, clothes and headbands.

Martha was entering fourth grade this year. She was nervous about a new teacher and new classmates, but excited about science experiments and the ability to check out three library books each time instead of two. She saw school supply shopping as a time to get yummy 'office' supplies and satisfactorily check off each item on her list.

Forty-five minutes later Anna had successfully cleared the check-out line, making sure Lucy hadn't added anything superfluous to the conveyor belt. She and the girls headed to the car, feeling harried but productive.

Anna drove them to a fast food restaurant for a rewarding lunch. Unfortunately, all the other mothers had done the same thing. They finally managed to get their food and squeeze into a recently vacated booth. Lucy ate hurriedly in order to go to the play area. Anna and Martha ate leisurely. Enjoying her new size ten body and hoping for even smaller, Anna ate a grilled chicken salad. Martha sucked on a strawberry shake and enjoyed the waffle fries and nuggets. Oh, to be eight again!

Sipping her diet Sprite, Anna sighed, "I think we left the house a couple of days ago. I can't believe it's only 11 o'clock."

Martha frowned, "We left this morning around nine."

Anna smiled. Martha was always such a concrete thinker. "I know, I was just being sarcastic."

"What?"

"I was just exaggerating. I meant it felt like we'd been out for days."

"Oh."

293

"I'm gonna have to nickname you 'Literally Martha.'"

"What does that mean?"

"'Literally' means you take everything exactly how it is--not at all figuratively."

Martha continued to frown. Anna tried again. "It means you don't see any gray areas--everything is black and white."

"But I don't see everything in black and white."

"No, I didn't mean--I know you see colors...Oh, never mind."

Anna returned to her salad and Martha picked up another fry. Lucy flitted between their booth and the play place.

"So, Momma, are you writing another book?" asked Martha.

"Well, yes, actually. You know I took my short stories and shaped them into a chapter book. The idea is if the book sales go well I'll put out a sequel."

"The main character is based on me, isn't it?" Martha asked proudly.

"Yep, and I need new ideas, so you better keep doing interesting things."

Martha looked concerned.

"Honey, I'm kidding. But I do want you to keep being my editor."

"Sure!"

On the drive home Anna contemplated her conversation with Martha. She was still trying to get used to the idea of being a writer--a real writer! The funny thing was that her writing had caused her to change her attitude about being a mother and homemaker, too. She now saw all the funny things, conversations, irritations, chaos and even the mundane as inspiration for her writing. Their lives gave meaning to her writing, and her writing gave meaning to their lives.

Anna and the girls stumbled into the house toting bags of school supplies.

"Just drop it all over here. We can sort it out later," directed Anna.

The girls dumped their packages and ran up to their rooms. Anna had just plopped onto the sofa when Martha yelled, "Momma, come quick!" Something in the tone of her voice sent Anna dashing upstairs.

"What--" Anna reached Martha's doorway and immediately saw the problem: her ant farm had been knocked over and ants ran in all directions.

"I'm so sorry, Momma," gushed Martha. "One of the cats or Max must have knocked it off the bookcase. What do we do? Can we somehow save them?" she asked, cupping her hands lovingly around a scattering of ants. Before Anna could respond, Martha drew back her hand shouting, "Ouch! They bit me!" All of Martha's protectiveness fled as she began squashing the ants left and right. Anna and Lucy joined in. Max crept upstairs and peered down the hall to see what the racket was. The three ladies looked like they were performing some deranged River dance.

Awhile later, giggling and exhausted, Anna once again plopped on the sofa.' 'Well,' she thought, 'there's another chapter in my next book--'The Carpenter Ant Massacre.'

Martha rushed into the room, eyes bright and shining. "Hey, Momma, now that my ants are gone, maybe I can send off for those butterflies!" She ran back upstairs, no doubt to unearth the butterfly growing kit she'd shoved in the closet ages ago. All she had to do was send off for the caterpillars to begin her next 'experiment.' Anna sighed.

A few moments later Martha descended the stairs looking deflated. "I can't do the butterfly thing yet."

"Why not?"

"Because I read the instructions, and it says ages 9 and up on the box. I won't be 9 for five months."

Anna laughed and hugged her daughter. She was half tempted to agree with her, just to postpone another insect experiment. "Oh, my Literally Martha'. It's okay, you can still send off for the caterpillars. You don't have to be 9--that's just the recommended age."

"Really?! Thanks, Momma!"

.... Charlotte and Barbara laughed as Anna regaled them with the story of the demise of the ant farm. The Enlightened Ladies once again occupied their table at the coffee shop. School had started, and the women no longer had to accommodate all their kids at the meeting. After the chuckles die down, the women sat quietly a moment, sipping tea and coffee.

"You know," Charlotte said finally, "I think we're suffering from summer vacation hang-overs."

297

"You can say that again," agreed Barbara. "Between pool parties, sleep-overs, amusement parks..."

"Yeah," continued Anna, "and ninety degree temperatures with one hundred percent humidity, and days where the sun is up from 7 a.m. to 9:30 at night..."

"And sticky, drippy popsicles and sippy cups full of milk that roll under the front seat of my car and begin to smell..." Charlotte paused, realizing the other two women had stopped nodding. "Well, I guess that's just me."

Anna and Barbara laughed.

"Do you guys realize it was only last fall that we all started meeting?" asked Barbara.

"My goodness, that's right! It seems longer," said Charlotte. "I mean,...I didn't mean, Oh, you know what I mean!"

"We've truly come full circle, from one fall to the next....but what a year of changes!" noted Anna.

Barbara inquired, "So, Anna, any more of your grandmother's wisdom to share?"

"You know, unless there are more writings at my mom's house or something, I think I've read them all."

"Now that you have an 'in' with a publisher, you should have Annie McDowell's work published!" suggested Charlotte.

"Hey, that's an idea," agreed Barbara. "You could flesh it out a bit if need be with advice of your own."

"I never thought of that. It would be an incredible way of honoring her and how she helped all of us," said Anna.

"Seriously, think of all we've done in our own lives that we may never have tried," reminded Charlotte.

"I would never be running my own catering business," admitted Barbara.

"I'd never be doing all this great work with animals, that I love," agreed Charlotte.

"And I would never be a writer. I'd still be overweight, complaining to anyone who'd listen about how I didn't know what I wanted to do with my life," added Anna, "and now--" She stopped, abruptly, glancing at her friends.

"What is it?" asked Charlotte, looking concerned.

"Well," hesitated Anna, "I've got some news."

"Another book?"

"You're moving!"

"No," grinned Anna, "I'm pregnant."

www.ingramcontent.com/pod-product-compliance
Lightning Source LLC
Chambersburg PA
CBHW060952030726
47503CB00003B/845